Christmas Ball

A Mermaid Story

C. L. SAVAGE

Mermaid Adventures

Book 4+

A SeaRisen LLC Publication
2016

Christmas Ball – A Mermaid Story

Authored by C. L. Savage
https://www.facebook.com/clsavagemermaids/

Edited by Miriam Ball

Published by SeaRisen LLC
– Boulder Colorado
http://searisen.com/
https://www.facebook.com/SeaRisen/

Cover Design by Mirela Barbu
– https://99designs.com/profiles/1328241

Paperback: ISBN 978-0-9909258-4-2
E-book: ISBN 978-0-9909258-5-9

Printed in the United States of America

First SeaRisen LLC Printing December 2016

10 9 8 7 6 5 4 3 2 1

To friends, old and new...

Table of Contents

Author's Note

November 26, 2016

Dear reader,

The third book in the Mermaid Adventures (M3) series is taking even longer to write than I'd hoped, and at best it'll be summer 2017 before it is published. To tide us over with some mermaid love, how about a Mermaid Christmas story? With M3 delayed, I took a quick break from writing it to bring to you this short story.

Because all my stories (to date) take about a week of my characters' lives, a Christmas Story on that timeline would be after book 20 or so. That is unrealistic, and everyone would be lost if I attempted that. So, after book 4 (M4) is where I decided to place this story. This means that M4 will take place during the characters' first semester of high school. I've had ideas while writing M3 on how M4 will go, and projecting those through the end of M4 is how I've come up with this story. Though I'll not be using any of the plot elements from M4 (I haven't even thought of them yet) here, I do know some things. For example, the characters enter high school and I know who some of those people in their lives will be. I've not introduced any more mermaid abilities than what is seen in book 3, which of course hasn't been published as of this date yet. So, sorry for some spoilers contained within.

There's no preface. This short story is more for the fans of the Mermaid Adventures series who are anxiously awaiting book 3.

Anyway, I do hope you enjoy this.

Thanks to "Editing-Queen of ServiceScape.com" for a quick edit and to "alerim of 99Designs.com" for the cover art.

Merry Christmas,

The Mermaids & C. L. Savage

1

Oval Office

December 22nd

Bitter ice crystals circled dark blue eyes that resembled the bottom of the ocean. White mist formed in the chilly air, blowing over cold hands. The lights flickered overhead. A pair of voices muffled by the whistling wind tickled the ears, the sentries changing posts.

The wind settled, the billowing snow cleared, revealing many dark figures crouching low against the wind, running forward with rifles borne on shoulders. Shock kept him from making a sound. In seconds their defenses overrun. More came after them. Nobody seemed to notice him.

Daring not to breathe as the first of many soldiers lurched past, darkness hiding their features. Only the wind-frozen snow breaking under boots spoke of their presence, then they were gone like ghosts. He held still. It was too late to shout an alarm. They were here and by, then he was alone. He thought to hear battle, instead stillness. Ice crystals carried on the wind swept around him and chilled him to the bone, but he dared not move. The baleful predawn moon stared down on the seemingly tranquil landscape, the snow broken in narrow trails. It was impossible to tell how many had passed.

A cough, the crunching of snow, coat blown open, forgotten, attention arrested by the uncertain figure sitting horseback, at once familiar. They were close, though he couldn't remember where they'd met before. Behind him sat others, officers he was certain. Why the mounts? Horses would be good for rugged terrain, but were rarely used in field exercises anymore. Most looked to the old friend, but nobody said anything. Behind them, crouched in the snow, were hundreds of figures. Blowing snow caused them to appear and disappear, hiding their numbers.

Running figures coming up the beaten-down snow path caught their attention. The news they'd been waiting for was carried on the heels of the runners. Even the horses lifted their heads, expecting that they'd finally get moving.

A warm hand slipped into his, drawing him out of the freezing moment. The trim figure of his wife leaned in, exchanging a kiss. "Come in," she urged. The shock of reality broke the icicles in his heart. He dared not look around.

"In a minute," he promised, not even meeting her gaze, hoping beyond hope he could return to the dream that was no dream. Her hand withdrew and she was gone, blown snow returning him to the meeting in the freezing morning.

"Sir!"

He spun, but it was only the runners. "She comes." Up the trail ran three women, bountiful hair flowing, bare legs, arms exposed to the cold. He thought for a second that he'd lost the moment, thinking himself on spring break his first year of college. His friends around him. The woman that had challenged them to volleyball in the lead. He'd not thought about her since then. She hadn't changed, nor did she see him standing in the snow. His office shoes offered no comfort in the cold, and yet she was barefoot, as were her companions. The weather not bothering them. They stopped before the familiar rider.

At that moment, the morning birds began their chorus, as if on cue at her appearance. The horizon lit by an orange burn, but the sun's warmth didn't reach them here.

"So we're ready?" spoke the familiar, yet unfamiliar friend. The watcher tried placing him, knowing for certain he'd never heard the man before, yet they'd had so many conversations. *How?* he puzzled absently, watching the tableau unfold.

"You and your descendants will keep the pact?"

"Yes," his friend said. The friend thought he had the better of the bargain. The watcher felt like that was an important moment, yet he too couldn't figure it out. Having spent his life in negotiations, spoken contracts were the most binding. Often having hidden, though sometimes pleasant outcomes. "We'll keep your secret," the friend said. Then he suddenly added, "Though I want to be able to call on you."

"Speak to water, and if we're able – we'll come." It wasn't quite the answer his friend wanted. The watcher knew that his friend gained in the exchange. Yet what it could mean escaped him, and he looked confused. The restless rustle of his men hidden behind him made him agree with a nod. "Ok then, come." She and her girlfriends turned, jogging off over the packed snow.

The riders followed, then columns of men and equipment

poured after. He was watching an army on the march. God there were so many of them, and so ill-equipped. Most didn't even have proper winter gear. The general in charge of them should be fired.

Pristine wilderness broke on a wide river. Hordes of men followed the three women out of the trees. Yet when the women walked into the river, the watcher couldn't quite believe what he was seeing. He thought the women pretty crazy to be running around in swimsuits in the middle of winter, but to see them swim into a freezing river was another thing. A massive fog rose from the river. The officers got off their mounts and whispered commands. Hidden by the fog, the women led the men, their mounts and artillery down into the river. His friend remained ashore until the last of them disappeared. No ripples disturbed the surface, but somewhere below, an army marched. The man watched the fog-shrouded river, thinking at any moment they'd return. They never did.

Turning, he shook off the cold, glad he didn't have to face walking into a frigid river. Instead, he walked into a warm room and went quickly for the fireplace. Halfway across the room he stopped, arrested by the painting over the fireplace. It was the man on horseback. No wonder he looked familiar. He'd had numerous conversations with the friend, all in his mind, one-sided, imagining the first president's words. Foremost in the painting was George Washington, the day he crossed the Delaware.

Spinning on his heel, the man walk quickly to the shelves and pulled down a much worn leather-bound journal. Passed down from president to president, it was Washington's personal notebook. Most of it contained Washington's observations on cabinet members, how to read men and so on. Flipping it open he scanned the laminated pages until he came to an entry that had never made much sense before.

> Myrtle Sea Bridesmaids turn tides, time and again. Aide invaluable, deep sights. Never trusted the brides, yet they've never failed. They've only ever helped when I've called. But their purposes are their own. They've never declared themselves for the Republic, or against the Enemy.
>
> The bargain struck, when I was most desperate. Our need was great, or I'd not have done it. And I thought I had the upper hand. Somehow Myrtle knew I'd be a father, though I never would father any. I've been called a father of this new nation. Sometimes I lie awake at night and wonder at what I have done. I do hope it was worth it.

This entry was so different from Washington's letters. This seemed to ramble. And below it was an artistic figure of a fish and woman combined, which to his eyes could only be a mermaid. Following it were a couple of instructions, though they were very smudged, as if water had poured over them many times, prior presidents having spilled on the pages. It's just one of many reasons they were preserved now. But only the first line had made any kind of sense, yet with what he'd learned tonight, the second now did.

1. Pour water into a basin, it helps to let the water still.
2. Unintelligible handwriting…
3. Be alone, or they won't answer.

Above the rim of the book was a Steuben glass pitcher of water on a silver tray along with several similar glasses. Placing the journal on his desk, he returned to the tray and set the glasses aside and carried the tray to the desk. As he lifted the pitcher, he was interrupted by a knock, then his body man entered. "Sir, you've got a call waiting for you."

"Alright. Thanks Stanley."

2

Tree Hunting

"So you think the tree is going to fall in that direction?" Coach Arden said, pointing down the hill.

"Coach, it would have, had you started cutting already. But the wind is picking up. Now, unless all the birds in sky land on this side, it's going to go the other way. At least, unless you put a diagonal cut in this side. That might change things. What do you think Melanie?" Lucy asked.

"Huh?" Melanie looked up from her phone. "Did you need me to move?"

"No, never mind. Anyone else want to weigh in?" Lucy looked pointedly at Jill, who shook her head, then to Cleo.

"I think Ri'Anne's going to be upset that we cut another tree down."

"We've been through all that," Lucy said. "The girl cries when the trees lose their leaves in the fall. Let alone a tree coming down for a perfectly good cause."

"I think we should consult her," Cleo said, defending her friend. She looked around for support. Ri'Anne wasn't there to save the tree.

"We're giving these to the homeless shelters," Jill said. "Ri'Anne will get over it. Besides, I already smoothed the way with her. I promised I'd plant seedlings when spring comes to replace them. You can help, if it'll make you feel better. I could use the help. Uncle, go ahead and cut. I don't think it matters which way it falls. It's only five feet tall or so."

"It helps to be precise," Lucy said, but eventually she nodded to Coach Arden and pointed a finger along the slope. He moved from his position, revved up the motor on the chainsaw and bent to the task of falling that tree.

The tree fell exactly where Lucy pointed, just as she'd predicted. *Too much brain power in that skinny frame,* Melanie thought. Of all their friends, Lucy was the only one without a super secret, but she more than made up for it in smarts. Nor did she ever complain about it. She was always just enjoying their little expeditions whenever they occurred. Ri'Anne liked to include her the most often, even though Lucy didn't have a conservation bone in her.

"Who's turn is it to carry it down to the truck?" Coach asked, shutting off the chainsaw.

"Jill and I got the last one," Cleo said.

"And I got the one before that," Melanie said. *Mermaid extraordinaire and Christmas-Tree tugboat.*

"Without my help, Coach wouldn't know which way to point the chainsaw."

"I'm sure I could figure it out on my own, Lucy," Coach Arden chimed.

Melanie could imagine the dark clouds over Lucy's head as she turned to the fallen Christmas tree. Lucy tried picking up the tree, but she struggled. "Someone help me!" Coach looked to Melanie. Technically, it would be her turn next. With a sigh she moved to her friend. "There really should be benefits to being a tree-lugger," she said.

"There are," Cleo said, putting a hip into Melanie's, causing her to stumble sideways. "We're helping the homeless." She then bent and took Melanie's spot and hauled the tree away with Lucy.

"I've had my fill of helping people," Melanie complained. Pulling at her collar she loosened her scarf. She was covered head to heels in chic "human" clothes. They looked pretty, cute and adorable, but she was uncomfortable. Plus, a storm was coming. She could feel it to her toes, and the thought of facing it as anything but a mermaid was unbearable. Melanie couldn't wait for summer again, or to get back to the gym. It was about the only place she felt normal. Up here in the mountains was too close to the sky for her.

"We've got this," Jill said, coming alongside. "If you want to go."

Jill wanted to take her friend into her arms, but after last summer things hadn't returned to the way they used to be before Melanie left for the South Pacific. After a second, Melanie nodded, turned and walked downhill. Not quite in the direction of the truck, but towards the closest water. After all the stories and daring escapades she had heard about Melanie, handcuffed, tied up and imprisoned, Melanie had to have grown a thick skin.

"So, which way should I cut this next one?" Arden asked, interrupting Jill's thoughts.

"What?" Jill sniffled, sucking in a load of snot. "Oh, I don't know Uncle. Away from you and me." Dragging her toe, Jill looked downhill.

"You crying?"

"No," Jill denied, hastily brushing tears from her face.

"How long are you going to let that go on? You have to go after her. Apologize to her."

"What for?!" Jill said. "It's Melanie that's been cold to me." But she knew her uncle wouldn't drop it until she at least attempted it.

The others returned, looked around and then found Coach Arden to move onto the next tree.

3

Clouds Speak

Unconsciously, Melanie wandered. There were so many emotions swirling inside of her that she didn't know where she was going, and she didn't care. She'd hoped, prayed that Jill would say something, anything other than saying Melanie wasn't needed. She'd almost transferred out on the spot, but then Coach Arden would have seen. The magic entity that now lived with her, whom she had named Ripple, had begun to wrap itself about her. All she had to do was allow Ripple to fully appear and she'd have been gone through the pathway. But there wouldn't have been anything on the other side, just emptiness. Just like her heart. The fuller the heart, the more room it seemed to have. When it was empty, Melanie didn't want anyone or anything, and it refused to fill on its own.

The slope grew steep, the snow deep. Walking along the edge, she sought a way down. Melanie was tempted to ride down the slope on her butt, but there were enough rocks poking up through the snow to dissuade her. Seeing deer making their way down a narrow trail ahead, Melanie called out to them for help, wondering if her magic would even work out of water, dressed as she was. The trail was too steep to navigate on her own.

Most of the time she was restricted magically from using her powers, but sometimes things worked in spite of Melanie's best efforts to understand. Her swimsuit was a magical creature that had bound itself to her. It could work when Melanie couldn't. It's how she'd almost transferred before.

The blowing snow cleared for a second, and she had a zoomed in moment to see the deer turn. People dressed in white from the waist up and brown below turned to look at her from atop the deer's backs. Then the vision was gone and she was seeing only two rather large bucks, both with rather large racks of antlers. They turned to look down, and Melanie called out, "Wait!" and rushed towards them, her feet almost sure. The snow didn't trouble her, but hidden stones tripped her up several times.

"Mistress," the lead buck said to Melanie. "What can we do for you?" The other scraped back snow with its foreleg and bent to eat the revealed grass.

They were huge, their shoulders meeting the top of her head. Big brown beautiful eyes smiled kindly. Her reaction to its size seemed to humor it. Melanie wondered how many people had thought that. Then she remembered the brief vision. She looked around, and then attuned. She saw them then, two women kneeling in the snow, hiding their brown leggings. Her eyes refused to see what was right in front of her.

"Elves?" Melanie said aloud, trying to deny what her sight told her. She'd seen so many things in the last six months, though, it was hard to be stunned, but stunned she was.

"I told you it was useless to try and hide from her," said the first woman, standing. She came out around the second deer, trailer her hand on the tremendous beast's flank. The other woman followed. "Sea lords see everything. I knew it was only a matter of time before a meeting."

"You know me?" Melanie asked.

"Not specifically," the second woman said. Her blonde hair poked out of her white stocking cap. "We've never met, or seen you before, personally. Though it's known that magic has been on the rise. So, we've known *of* you. It's actually why we're here."

Stepping around her friend, the woman looked up at Melanie. They were miniature sized women, she only come up to Melanie's chin. "Are you The Sea Lord?"

"The Sea Lord?" Melanie wondered aloud. "You must mean Jill. She's back that way," she hooked her thumb over her shoulder the way she'd come.

"You've offended her," the first said. She had rosy cheeks. So, Melanie nicknamed them Rosy and Blonde, for they otherwise looked so much alike that they could be twins. Rosy came forward and took Melanie's hand. "We're sorry. We didn't mean to. We're sensitive to others' emotions, but we're not very good at being sensitive in return."

Too late, Melanie wanted to say. Tears came to her eyes but she banished them, using her powers to absorb the water. She hadn't thought there was more room to be hurt. Apparently, there was infinite room for hurt in empty hearts. Maybe she would take that transfer with Ripple down. If it goes nowhere, then she'll be there a while.

The two women shared a look. "Take Belfast," Blonde suggested.

"Hmm?" Melanie barely registered the suggestion. It was

only the odd name that perked her curiosity.

Rosy turned back to the deer, then pulled reins out of a pocket, drew the halter over the deer's head, then led the animal around to Melanie. "This is Belfast," the elf said. She put the reins in Melanie's hands. Instantly a bond formed between the deer and Melanie. She was in the mind of Belfast, and the proud buck greeted her again. The love in the creature poured through the connection, pushing into the emptiness in her heart.

"Hi," Melanie almost cooed to Belfast, feeling silly and girly for the first time in… she couldn't remember how long. "Wow, you're beautiful," she said putting her hand on his snout.

Blonde touched Melanie's hand, "Though of course, you probably don't need the harness." Melanie nodded. It was true. She could talk with animals, but this connection was so much better.

Tearing her eyes away from Belfast's eyes, Melanie realized her cold heart had made her callus in return. "Are you sure? I have other ways of getting about."

Blonde shook her head, "We can ride double. Besides, our meeting may have been chance, or it might not have. Your guidance has saved us from going down there." Melanie knew she meant the city in the far distance. "It's not the easiest thing to be among humans for us." It wasn't that easy for Melanie either, but she didn't say that. Life had all sorts of difficulties, but this encounter had perked up her spirits. She'd not dump more troubles on them. "If you can, be sure Belfast gets home alright. Not anytime soon, though. He'd like it if you kept him for a bit."

"The lucky swine," the other deer said as Melanie climbed

up on Belfast. A giggle rose up in Melanie and she couldn't help but laugh all the way down the slope. It felt like an iceberg lifted from her chest. How long had it been since she'd laughed?

If it weren't for the snow and Melanie keeping her eyes on the invisible trail Belfast followed, she would have noticed the clouds above acting funny. At first they thinned, directly over her, and then began to roll back and forth like water.

"Hello?" a voice thundered. Snow fell from all the trees around Melanie and Belfast skidded sideways, saving them from being doused in an avalanche. He was connected to her senses and she was to his.

"Not so loud," Melanie said before she'd really looked to the source. It wasn't anything like she'd imagined. In the sky above, she saw, through drifting snowflakes, a man from a little over waist high, wearing a suit and tie, looking down on her. She recognized what he was doing. Speaking to water, he'd contacted her. He looked familiar, though Melanie was fairly certain she'd never shared the trick with a man before. So, she wasn't sure. "Come down here," Melanie commanded, but it didn't work. She knew her coat blocked her. Pushing back a sleeve, she reached up and gave a tug. The water he used allowed her to grab onto it. The giant man and his water came down until she was looking at him normal sized and upright, instead of him looming over her. It still left him at an odd angle, because he still seemed to be looking down on her.

"You're riding a deer," the now familiar face said.

Melanie wasn't quite sure what to say in response, but what she said sorta surprised her. "Very perceptive. This is Belfast." Then she patted the deer and said, "Belfast, this is President MacLeod."

"Very nice to meet you," Belfast said, but Melanie didn't expect the man to understand him. And she was right, but he did see that Belfast understood her.

"He said 'Hi' didn't he?"

"It's the polite thing to respond in kind," Melanie said, hardly believing she was talking to this man in such a way. She knew admirals, but this was the leader of her country, and here she was giving him lessons in etiquette. And he was affronted, too. It was obvious he wasn't used to being corrected. *Well done, Melanie. You're on a roll at turning friendships into dust.* But then, there was a reason he was the leader. He knew how to make amends.

"I'm sorry. You're right. Nice to meet you Belfast."

Belfast understood through Melanie and gave him a bow, tilting his head down with bent leg. *Hey, no genuflections required.* But Melanie didn't get a chance to tell Belfast.

"Ok, well. If that's not the most peculiar thing I've ever seen. I can't believe I'm having this conversation. Are you who I think you are?"

"Who were you expecting?" Melanie asked, thinking the man wanted Jill's mother Goldie from the image in his mind. But she dismissed the thought. He also had President Washington in his mind too.

"Myrtle?" and he shook his head at Melanie's blank look. He meant the blond woman, so he definitely meant someone who wasn't Goldie. "If I wasn't already out on a limb with all of this, you're a sea maid?"

"I've not heard us described like that, but there are so many odd things in the world. What's one more?"

His eyelashes blinked a dozen times rapidly. Melanie wondered what he was thinking. "Is there any chance we can talk, in a normal way?"

"I certainly could use a trip," Melanie said. "Where shall I meet you?"

"Um, that's going to be difficult. I don't suppose you have a ball gown with you?"

Melanie clenched her teeth in a grimace, at first caught off guard by the question, but she quickly realized that in so many ways that would be difficult. Her swimsuit might be enough. The fish always resembled a gown when she swam in the sea, but she really didn't want to be the Cinderella to his Prince, especially via magic.

There was a noise behind him. Melanie heard voices. He looked away, nervously, and she drew her hand down from where she'd held onto the magic he was using. It was hers to use, and she cut the connection.

"He was inviting us to a ball, and you hung up on him!" Belfast critiqued. "We're going to be missing the elvish Winter Ball – they're always the best. You have to get him back."

Mouth open, Melanie listened to Belfast's tirade. "You like balls? There's so much dressing up to do, and if you get to dance, and I mean a big if, the guy dances on your feet the whole time."

"I do not. I'm a good dancer. I'm taking you to this ball. I'll show you," Belfast said proudly. "Now open the way, you have to get dressed."

"I don't have a dress," Melanie said, but Ripple jumped out of her collar and opened a pathway. It wanted to go to the ball too. The view through the new portal was of the grassy fields outside the White House. "No. Are you crazy? They'll kill us." She'd already wrestled with marines before. Taking on over-protective president guards wasn't her idea of a good time. "How about the river near the Washington Monument? That gives us a way out if we need it." Ripple changed the view to the dark Potomac.

"I can't swim that well!" Belfast said, balking at riding into the midst of the river. Again the view changed, and they were looking at the shore beside the water. With a leap, Belfast charged through. He was so excited, almost cutting Melanie in half. She ducked to squeeze in under the top of the portal.

"Brrr, it's cold," Melanie complained. She rarely was affected by cold, and only wore what she did because it would be out of place to be in shorts or a t-shirt in the middle of winter. Not that most of her friends cared, wearing so little (and always freezing), but Melanie had a secret to keep.

"Hey, slow down!" Melanie chided as Belfast took off running up the hill, jumping fences. She'd never been to Washington, DC before. Everywhere she looked Christmas decorations flowed over an already ornate scene. It would be expected that the nation's capital would be manicured. The park Belfast cut across was no exception, but he wasn't staying to the sidewalks as any normal person would do, and they were getting a lot of attention.

A stone pillar rose into the sky, disappearing into thick clouds. "That's the Monument," Melanie told Belfast. "I wish it was clear, so we could see all of it." Feeling her magic rise at her thought, she clamped down on it. "Not now," she said. At least her magic listened to her, this time. Ripple so willing, it would have done something if it could. She really had to watch her words around this bunch. Belfast had them trotting across the lawn towards the well-lit White House. A line of cars were waiting to drive in.

"Slow down, please," Melanie begged. "We don't have an invitation."

"You have an invitation," Belfast corrected. "I heard President MacLeod ask if you had a dress."

"Yeah but, I don't. And no Ripple, I'm not doing magic, nor are you. In fact no magic any of you. I really don't want to be arrested and spend Christmas in a jail. Promise me, or we're turning around."

Melanie tugged on the reins. She hadn't touched them to guide Belfast since she mounted, but he stopped so short she almost went over his head and impaled herself on his antlers. He blew a great heap of steam tossing his head. She hated restraining him, he had gotten them so close to their goal. He couldn't take it, and gave in, which heaped guilt all over her for making him.

"We'll dance if we get in, ok?" Melanie promised him. "Ripple?"

Belfast was an adult deer, and had understood, but Ripple was a basically a child. It didn't really understand propriety. Though it was learning, there were things Ripple did that made her upset. It didn't like those times. This wasn't one of them, yet. It seemed to sense it, and told her, **I'll try.**

"Ok, thanks," she told them. "That still doesn't mean we'll get in. In a normal way," Melanie added, just in case either of them tried something that would get her in but wouldn't be magic. "They have to let us in on their own."

"Stay mounted," Belfast said, his hooves clopping on concrete. Cars skidded to a halt as they entered the street. But instead of heading straight for the gate, Belfast headed right, and then angled in behind the last car in line to enter the property. Heads hung out windows to catch a look at them. Then cameras turned from the gate.

"This is too much attention!" Melanie complained, but Belfast didn't move and she wasn't about to guide him again.

"What are you talking about?" Belfast said. "This is great. They love me. And if you'd unbend a little, add your magic to the night, you could be Cinderella."

"I'm already Cinderella," Melanie said. "I love my part in the play." *If only Jill could see it.* A dump truck of misery returned to spoil her mood. *If only Jill saw how wonderful this life was.* "I have the two of you, and all of this. What more do I need?" The words almost helped, but what Melanie wanted for Christmas was impossibly far away.

"You don't sound convincing."

"Yeah," Melanie admitted. "There's not much I can do about it, either. We're almost there. What are we going to do?"

"Let me do the talking," Belfast said.

"Um, ok, but you see they have guns, right?"

"Trust me."

"Need me to interpret?"

"I'm good."

"Okay…"

The news cameras were all trained on them. So far Melanie had managed to forget about them, engrossed in her conversation with Belfast. But now there were only two limos between them and the gate. Atop Belfast, Melanie was sticking out like a sore thumb, and the limo behind them had them well lit up. Melanie had thought it bad, but then there were no more cars before them, and Belfast trotted up to the gate.

4

Invitation

"Belfast, you're going to get me fired..."

"You have the honor of meeting Melanie, the Sea Lord," Belfast said.

"Yes but... No disrespect Sea Lord, but this is most unusual. Of course you're welcome wherever I have a say, and it's not like we don't plan for eventualities. Still, I'm so fired. You don't know. But I can't tell Belfast no. He's just too cute, don't you think? Who could tell those eyes no?"

Melanie couldn't believe it. An elf. This one not a tiny snow elf, either. The pretty woman was tall. But she let them pass, handing Melanie a card that she suspected was electronic. She'd fished it out of the guard shack.

"I don't have an extra guest pass. This should get you anywhere in the building. Please don't get me fired, ok?"

Like Melanie had made the others promise her not to make trouble, she had to do the same. Gulp. "I promise," she said. There wouldn't be a dance between her and the elf to make up for it either. "There any more…" A storm cloud appeared over the woman's head. Melanie shut up before she said, "elves?"

"Ooops," the elf confessed. "You two, move along, before I really lose it. A sea lord, a real sea lord…" the elf muttered as they pranced in, Belfast having decided that there weren't enough eyes focused on him yet.

"You promised no magic," Melanie rebuked him.

"I didn't. I swear. Elves are just so easy. If you weren't along, she'd have pulled the sugar cubes out instead of that inedible plastic card she gave you. I hope you like it," Belfast griped, lifting his chin and striding like a mighty stallion. It was a good thing he was being all indignant or Melanie would have noticed where she was and totally freaked out. Instead, she was apologizing and stroking his neck, trying to soothe his ruffled feathers. It wasn't until he came to a stop under the portico that she fell out of the saddle, as it were. The guys in perfect military dress uniforms managed to catch her before she did a face plant on the stairs and knocked her teeth out, like the total awesome heroes they looked like. If she wasn't already a klutz, she'd have swooned. Belfast trotted off before anyone could take the reins. He knew Melanie was going to give him advice, like stay off the grass and stuff, but he took off before she could say anything.

The soldiers set Melanie on her feet. She straightened up her outfit, but next to everyone else she was way underdressed, and there was mud on her boots. Beautiful Christmas music and tremendous heat oozed out the doorway around the line of people waiting to go in. Heat lamps above helped to alleviate the cold.

Out of the next car to unload, Melanie noticed the gowns, shoes and lack of coats. The women hustled up and squeezed in behind Melanie, but they were focused on their dates. Nobody was saying a word to her, which she was grateful for because instead of speaking *to* her, they'd be talking *about* her. She felt exactly as she looked, straight from a forest. The line bustled forward a few steps and she entered the building proper. Two marines held the doors, scanning her with curious eyes. She just smiled up at them. They made her feel like less of a kid. Merriment twinkled in their eyes. They were far closer to her age than any of the other guests.

They moved up again, and Melanie caught sight of the screening apparatus. Ooo, what was she going to do? She'd pass the screen, but they were asking questions. A woman, Melanie saw, was getting into an argument. *Nothing good is going to come of that. Just give them what they want.* But the woman couldn't hear Melanie's thoughts, so they all had to wait for her to be sorted out.

A sneeze followed by, "Too much perfume," got the woman in front of Melanie in trouble. But then she was out of the way and Melanie was greeted by two dopey eyes. "Aren't you cute!" Melanie said, bending to pet the Doberman.

"I suppose dashing or handsome is too much to ask for?"

Melanie ran her hands down his flanks, and pulled back a little, measuring. "Dashing."

"She's a pass," he said up to his handler.

Melanie caught the disapproval. "You're not supposed to pet him."

"But he's so cute," and at a bark, "and dashing."

"Well, Trigger likes you. Not many people pay him any attention."

"That's sad," Melanie told Trigger. "You're smelling people?"

"I've a good nose for trouble. Let me guess. You've been in pine woods?" At Melanie's nod of encouragement, he continued, "And been hunting?" He cocked his head, unsure.

Melanie was confused, then realized Trigger thought Belfast might have been a hunt. "No. I rode the buck Belfast here. He's out there somewhere."

"A buck, really? A deer is wandering the grounds? Haha, that's sure to get the pups in a tizzy. You come in style, Sea Lord."

"Can you move forward please? It's freezing out here!" called a guest at the back of the line.

I recognize that voice! "Sorry," Melanie called, getting back to her feet. It was clear right up to the guard at the scanner. "See you, Trigger."

"Back to smelling stinky perfume. Laters, Sea Lord. Thanks for talking with me."

"I.D. and invitation," the guard woman said to Melanie when she got there.

"Um," Melanie said, and then remembered the card the elf had given her. Digging into her pocket, she pulled it out.

The guard's eyebrow raised at seeing it. Then she pointed, "Employee entrance, over there." There was nobody even guarding that entry. She scanned the card and a little light above the red carpet blinked green. Without any formality, Melanie walked in. To the right were doors into offices, and to the left the party. She needed a guide, so Melanie returned to the security entrance on the party side.

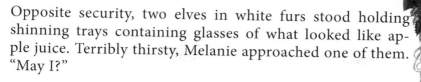

Opposite security, two elves in white furs stood holding shinning trays containing glasses of what looked like apple juice. Terribly thirsty, Melanie approached one of them. "May I?"

"Sure, but its…"

"I think the Sea Lord knows, don't you?" said the other elf.

"Knows what? And can you not call me Sea Lord where others can hear?" Melanie sipped the drink. Her nose told her before her mouth got a taste, but she wasn't listening. Her eyes tried to go through the top of her head, and heat rose up to her cheeks. "That's good!"

"Nobody can hear us. Elvish is a magical language, like your ability to speak with animals. Nobody hears you do that, right?"

"Unless they know the language," the elf beside Melanie said, "of course."

"Of course," the other said. They both gave each other a tiny bow, then turned to hand out drinks to newcomers.

So that explained a few things. How long had Melanie wondered about that particular trait? Lifting the glass to her lips, it was neatly plucked from her fingers before she could get more than a whiff. "Hey!" she turned, and an arm linked in hers and pulled her right into the party.

Admiral O'Burk said, "A good bubbly like this is wasted on the young." He smelled the drink, as Melanie should have done, then sipped from her glass. Melanie fumed, though she'd waited for him. The professor was enjoying her discomfort.

"Why are you here? Are you following me?" Melanie asked.

"My dear, I have an invitation. I don't think you do, do you?"

"I have this," Melanie waved the card, and he again plucked it from her fingers.

"Where did you get this?" he asked. After a second of thought, he returned the card to Melanie. "Keep it safe. That'll get you into about anywhere here. I cannot imagine where you got that."

"An elf gave it…" There was a sudden crash, glasses of champagne exploding on the marble floor. Melanie looked up to see a woman disappearing into thin air. *Had she transferred?* Then Melanie attuned and saw the elf standing there, furious with both herself and Melanie. She then turned and dashed through the guests, keeping up the invisible thing the snow elves in the forest had done. *That's got to be a great trick.*

Admiral O'Burk steered them away from the mess. He was so adept, Melanie didn't doubt he was a good dancer. He was so unconscious about his gentlemanly ways. Melanie automatically let herself be guided. It was really quite amazing. She was enjoying his company, for that alone. Though no doubt when they returned to school he'd pretend he didn't know her. It was too bad.

"Did you say elf?" he asked when they were away.

"You don't miss much."

"An elf?"

"Hush," Melanie said. "Before someone hears."

"You said it first."

"I was careless. I thought people knew," Melanie said. The way the waiter had acted, Melanie was sure that she'd spoken out of turn.

“Knew what?” the admiral wanted to know, but Melanie shook her head, refusing to speak any more. If she did, she was going to get the elves in trouble, and she'd promised not to do that. She decided to enjoy herself, at least until she bumped into the president. Then she was sure to make a mess of things again.

When he'd stopped prying with his eyes, Melanie asked, “Admiral, can we get some food?”

“I'd appreciate it if you called me Stacy.” He guided them out of the entryway and towards the smell of good things. Smelling brownies, she turned them about, accidentally taking control of their movement. But he was an easy partner, letting her guide them. She found the tray covered in sugary delights. A hand extended a plate from the other side, holding two tiny cubes with toothpicks. Melanie frowned, taking the plate and drooling over the abundance of full-size cuts on the glistening silver tray.

“The lady would like more,” Stacy said. The server read her and decided to use a wide knife to scoop her up one of the large delights.

“Wish I were young again,” a woman beside Melanie said, receiving a plate with only a couple brownie cubes. “These'll go straight to my waist. Careful they don't stick to your teeth. Chew with your back teeth, or gum them if you can.” Then she smiled her pearly whites and disappeared back into the crowd before Melanie could say thanks. The idea of chocolate sticking to her teeth almost made Melanie put the plate down. The out-of-this-world smell stayed her hand. She took one of the toothpicks and plucked the cube off with her lips. Her tongue got ahold of the taste, and she almost bit down.

Oh so good! "Divine!" Melanie gushed, water flooding her mouth. It was all she could do not to swirl the taste around and mash the cube. Instead, she sucked at the goo that was forming in her mouth until it dissolved into nothingness. The admiral led them to another table where he built a plate of real food snacks for her. Then did the same for himself. He took her brownies and dumped them on top of the food and discarded the extra plate. It was swept up a second later.

Before she could get another bite, she was interrupted. "Excuse me," spoke an official looking dude. He wasn't an elf, but he was dressed real nice. "Miss, there's someone I'd like you to meet."

5

Interview

"Can I come?" Admiral Stacy O'Burk asked, making sure the guard knew he was with Melanie.

"Of course, Admiral. This way."

"Do you know him?" Melanie asked, sure that she was about to be arrested. Stacy gave her a brief shake of his head. He'd taken her arm again, which made it difficult to eat. She wanted to gobble up everything, before they locked her away. "I think I'm in trouble."

"You think?"

"I have a way of getting into trouble."

"You'll find a way out, I'm sure. You always do. I don't suppose you have the Kraken in your pocket?"

"No, Ken went home for Christmas."

"Ken's the Kraken?"

"I have loose lips," Melanie laughed. She smiled up at her

guide, begging him with her eyes not to say anything. "You won't say anything to him, will you?"

"You're impossible."

"I know."

"What's going on there?" They'd stopped inside an office beside glass-paneled door. "Stay here," their escort said, but of course they naturally followed him out into the cold. Inside, they'd not heard the dogs barking. The "pups," as Trigger had called them, had Belfast cornered to their left, yelling at him. On the way out they passed a bucket of flowers. All the heads were missing except one beautiful red rose.

"Stay back," Stacy grabbed Melanie by the elbow as she charged out of his arm. "Such a beautiful animal, but they'll probably shoot it."

"They'll do no such thing!" Melanie broke free, pushing her way past the guy who'd guided them.

"Hey!" But Melanie ignored him. He grabbed her by the shoulder, and she dragged him after her, his business shoes sliding on the snow-covered porch area.

Belfast saw her, but he couldn't do anything. He was trapped. "You weren't kidding. These people are mad," he said. "I only ate a few roses."

"He ate them all," one of the dogs said. They all backed up as Melanie approached. Belfast had gotten his antlers caught in a lattice for vines, and he was in danger of tearing it down. Whatever flowers might have been upon it, gone.

"You could have *asked* for food," Melanie said, stepping beside him.

"I'm sorry," Belfast apologized.

Melanie picked up his reins off the ground and laid them over his neck before they too became tangled up on something. Then Melanie jumped up on him, landing on her hands and feet. Balancing with hands out wide, she stood up. "Hold still," she chided as he sidestepped a dog. "And all of you, back off. I've got this."

"We can't just leave," the guard dogs said, but they did sit and quieted. Their handlers approached, surprised at the sudden change.

"Hey, can we help?" Human guards stood to either side of Belfast. They'd had out weapons, but they were putting them away.

"I'm going to need pliers and maybe wire cutters," Melanie said standing on Belfast's head. "You really have a lot of sharp tips," she said to Belfast. "You're all snagged up." The wire was so tight, but she pulled anyway. If she didn't free Belfast soon, there might be more trouble. And she wanted to avoid that. A strand of wire came loose at Melanie's tug, and suddenly she was windmilling her arms and falling.

"Sir, you should stay back."

"Stacy!" But it wasn't the admiral who caught her. Melanie was looking up into a bemused and pained face. She wasn't a lightweight kid anymore. The man said nothing of it, though, and set her to her feet with the help of a truckload of people standing at his back, keeping him from going down too. It took her a couple seconds to recognize the president from the man she'd seen in the water. He looked different and very well dressed. The suit and tie he'd been wearing before paled to this finery. "God, I'm so sorry," Melanie brushed snow from where it fell on him.

"Nonsense. So you came. I'm glad to see you."

"Belfast insisted. He thought you'd implied an invitation. He likes balls. I've promised him a dance."

"And I mean to have that dance, if I can ever get untangled." Belfast's neck muscles tightened, but Melanie put her hand on him to restrain his impulse to rip free.

"Belfast?" President MacLeod asked, even though they'd met before. Maybe he asked because of the others. He was sharp not to give it away. Stacy had snuck up to stand beside him. The admiral's eyes were curious to hear what Melanie would say.

Melanie's mouth went through the motions before she finally thought the truth would be best. "This is Belfast," she gestured to the tangled up deer.

"He's beautiful." A stunning woman stepped through the others. The president's daughter. *Ah!* Melanie hadn't realized she was behind the president. *I should know her name*, Melanie thought. Then it came to her, *Heather*. She was twenty-something and looked gorgeous. Behind her stepped several of her friends, all neatly done up. She was in college, Melanie felt certain. Home for Christmas. Heather put her hand on her father's arm then stepped towards Belfast, but one of the many followers stepped between them.

"There's so many people," Belfast said. "I'm tame and all, but they're making me nervous." Melanie heard the tension in his voice. "I don't suppose you could send them away like you did with the hounds?" They were indeed backed away.

"Um sure," Melanie reached out to Stacy. He stepped to her side, but he had eyes only for the great deer at her back. "Can you send them away? They're making Belfast nervous."

"Them?" Stacy asked, looking around, not seeing what she was talking about.

"I think she means us," President MacLeod said. "Go on in everyone. You too, dear," he said to Heather when she protested. "I'll be right along." Of course, if he wasn't leaving the brigade around him wasn't leaving either. "Alright I'm going."

"You just sent away the president of the United States in his own home," Stacy said.

"I didn't. Belfast did."

"Here are the tools you requested ma'am," said one of the guards who'd asked to help.

"Thanks." Turning about she saw the elf guard from the entrance guard shack. A number of elves were with her. They'd gathered to watch. Giving her the eye, Melanie gave her a look when she approached. "Can you get him free?" she pleaded of the elf, passing the tools to her. "Thanks."

"You really are trying to get me fired." But she agreed and called over her friends. Together they surrounded Belfast. He held still as they worked on freeing him.

"Don't forget your promise," Belfast called after Melanie as she turned, tucking her arm into Stacy's.

"I won't," she said, promising again.

"She's so going to get me fired," Melanie heard the elf guard grumble as they walked away. She couldn't help but crack a huge smile. Stacy led them to a door near where they'd exited from the building. Someone there opened it for them and they entered a well-known room, seen from dozens of movies and television shows. The guard was worried about being fired? Well, Melanie knew how she felt. This was not going to go well, she was sure of it.

There was only the president waiting for them. He spoke up, "Thank you Admiral O'Burk, thank you. But I'm going to insist you wait outside."

"He knows about me," Melanie said.

"That makes one of us. Stacy, please, I must insist."

"It's ok Melanie. I'll be in the office over there," and he pointed to their right. There were a number of doors leading out. "Come find me when you're done." Stacy left, closing the door behind him. A nervous sigh came from the man at her back.

"Do you know why you're here?" the president asked when Melanie had turned around. He stood at his desk, where a tray lay. She could see water on it, and next to it crystal glasses and a half empty pitcher. "I'm not quite sure what to do with it," he admitted. "Nobody's been in here since then."

"A towel?" Melanie suggested, coming up beside him.

"Right," but his eyes widened as Melanie put her hand to the water in the tray, and the water ran into her. In a moment the water was gone. She put her hand to the top of pitcher, and what had been in the tray ran out of her fingers into the glass vessel.

"I think I'm going to have a seat," President MacLeod said, and he sat on one of the couches in the room. When he'd gathered himself, "What are you?" he asked.

"Most would call us mermaids," Melanie said.

"But not all?"

"Our formal title is Sea Lord."

"I suppose that is why you have an admiral on your arm? Because I'm quite certain that Admiral O'Burk never married. He retired and took up teaching in a little town in Colorado."

Melanie shrugged, what was there to say? She'd not asked him to do that. "He said he was invited. But no, I didn't rope him into being my escort."

"You can do that?"

"He insisted," Melanie said, sidestepping the question. She never used her mermaid powers to make people do things for her. That seemed wrong. Sea creatures, on the other hand, were more than willing to do whatever she suggested.

"Forgive me. Onto the reason I called. Can you hand me that book on the table?" Melanie passed him an old leather bound book. It didn't have a formal binding, but it looked to be a collection of old paper, notes and other things stuffed into a leather wrap. He flipped it open to a page, and said, "Here, read this. What do you make of it?"

Myrtle Sea Bridesmaids turn tides, time and again. Aide invaluable, deep sights. Never trusted the brides, yet they've never failed. They've only ever helped when I've called. But their purposes are their own. They've never declared themselves for the Republic, or against the Enemy.

The bargain struck, when I was most desperate. Our need was great, or I'd not have done it. And I thought I had the upper hand. Somehow Myrtle knew I'd be

a father, though I never would father any.
I've been called a father of this new nation. Sometimes I lay awake at night and wonder at what I have done. I do hope it was worth it.

"It was written by George Washington."

"So that's why you called me Myrtle. I was wondering. Not a very trusting sort, was he? History doesn't make him out to be conniving. I wonder if this is really the President Washington."

"It's him. Before I contacted you, I had a vision. The night he crossed the Delaware, just before a series of victories that turned the war with the British, General Washington met three women who I believe helped him and most of his forces cross the river that Christmas Eve in exchange for a deal – to keep your kind secret. Kind of long-reaching for anyone, but Washington was desperate. The American forces were about to collapse, and he needed some victories to rally support. Without the aid of your people that night, it's possible the revolution would have failed."

"Why tell me this?" Melanie was floored to be learning these things.

"I like history, mostly. And I don't put much stock in visions. This one seemed verifiable. Have I had others? Yes. Never before taking office, but many since. There's a mantle that has descended upon me. It changes you to be a leader. I never really experienced that as a senator, or on my home city's council."

"I understand authority," Melanie said.

"And yet you sneak into my party?"

"I came in through the front gate, and I think you were going to invite me. Am I right?"

"Well, then, we better get you fixed up."

"Do you want this back?" Melanie held up the book. "I'd like a copy of this page, if possible. It might help a friend of mine." Jill was researching mermaid history, and Melanie thought if she could get this to Jill it would go a long way towards healing their friendship.

"Yes. There's nothing sensitive on the page. Before the vision, I didn't know what to make of it. The instructions are incomplete otherwise," the president said, and then in a change of tone, asked, "How good are you with water?"

Melanie pointed her finger straight up and she projected a mini-fountain of water that splashed back onto her hand. She kept it up for a couple of seconds before putting her hand back in her coat pocket.

"Ok, wow. That's not what I mean. But that's really impressive."

"It's only a party trick," Melanie said. "Not much good except as a prank."

"Like a water gun?"

Melanie nodded. "Water is my friend, if that's what you're asking."

"No... Who'd ever think to ask that? I can tell you don't think in the box most of us like to call the normal world."

"There's nothing normal about it."

"Yeah, well, I can see that. You rode in on that deer then?"

"Belfast."

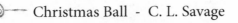

"And he's out there eating the flowers?"

"I'm not sure. I left him in the care of your elves."

"My what?"

"Um, I wasn't supposed to say anything. I'm so bad at this. Your handlers. You have those, right?"

"The dog handlers?" But at Melanie's confusion, "You mean like for a stable?" Melanie nodded yes. "We don't have stables here. At Camp David, yes. I wish we were there now."

Melanie thought fast on her feet, making it up as she went, feeling sweat on her back. "Your security people. I left Belfast with some of them."

"You called them elves."

"So I did," Melanie temporized. Hopefully she'd backpedaled far enough. Melanie's phone took that moment to beep from her back pocket. She pulled it out and read the screen. From Dad - *Melanie, where are you?*

"It's my father, wondering where I'm at. Can we take a selfie? He'd believe me, but a picture would help smooth the way."

"Don't you want to be wearing a ball gown first?"

"Yes of course, but I don't have one. And this is the Oval Office. It's not like I'll ever be standing in here again."

"Somehow I doubt it, but sure. Want to record it?" At Melanie's enthusiastic head nod, he got up off the couch and met her in front of his desk. "It's Melanie, right? We never shook hands and all that."

"Melanie McKenzie."

"McKenzie? Interesting. Ok, let's do this."

He put his arm around Melanie and she held out her phone and recorded them.

"Hi. I'm Tolvar MacLeod, and I'm here with Melanie McKenzie. Merry Christmas from the White House. That good?"

"Yes, thanks," Melanie said and edited out the end, then sent it off to her dad with the subject title, "You'll never guess where I'm at."

"I'm due at the party. It's past time I joined them. Now, let's get you that dress."

6

The Ball

Melanie's feet hurt. First Daughter Heather had graciously opened her wardrobe for Melanie to choose from. But Melanie didn't have a clue when it came to ball gowns. It wasn't the same as going to the prom. She picked a short skirt, something cute with flowers if she couldn't have fish.

But when Melanie came out with the hip hugger, "No!" Heather said, lecturing Melanie on propriety. "Princesses wear gowns, with skirts. You know. Picture Cinderella, Belle, any of them. When going to a ball we wear flowing things. Think of ocean currents, or waves cascading upon a beach. We flow. We don't splash!"

Melanie was stunned at the example, but since Heather clearly waited for her to say something, she said, "Flow, of course." It was fun being lectured by the woman on how the sea works. "I love the surf. Is there something like that in here? I'm not seeing it."

"There is. In the spare bedroom closet. I've not worn it since Dad was elected, and it's unlikely I'll ever wear it again. It's the opposite of a princess gown. You're all the wrong colors for a blue dress, though. I would think you'd want layered pinks, reds, golds and even a soft yellow would go great with your hair."

"Can we at least look at it?" Melanie was insistent that she look at the thing. It sounded perfect. She didn't want a princess gown.

"Ok, I'll get it…"

The woman was a cross between a fairy-godmother and Cinderella's sisters, but Melanie was determined to be kind. She was going out of her way to help Melanie when it was her party. Heather told her that her father threw them for her when she returned home for Christmas and how much fun they were.

It was one of the many perks of being president, Melanie supposed, to have glorious balls. While she waited, she removed her winter chic clothes she'd once loved. Looking in the mirror, she examined the magic swimsuit and the girl inside it. She'd changed so much since that day five months ago when she'd followed Jill into the pool to end up in the sea. The suit wasn't the same, made of different fish, and was imbued with Ripple's magic. But it was hers and had seen her through so many adventures. Outwardly she hadn't changed at all since saying yes to Jill and to water. But inwardly Melanie was a whole new person. She lifted her chin and spun about, facing the mirror as she spun. It was so much easier underwater to spin. But soon she'd be doing so on a dance floor.

Grabbing her belly, Melanie stopped her twirl and freaked out. She was going to a real ball, where people actually knew how to dance. They'd be good. It wouldn't be prom. That was both good and bad. Good because her partners wouldn't step on her feet, and bad because she'd have to match them. This wasn't prom where she could hide behind the seniors who all knew what to do, or pretended to, making a fool of themselves and drawing all the attention. If Melanie misstepped, she'd have all too much attention. She wanted to flee.

Hands aflutter, Melanie calmed herself. She already had a short dance card. Stacy would be nice, she hoped, helping her get her bearings. What did she know of the retired admiral though? Not much, not enough except that earlier he'd displayed gentlemanly ways. She could trust him to not embarrass her. Once she was comfortably hidden within the throng, nobody would see her.

Heather returned, interrupting Melanie's thoughts.

"That's a swimsuit. You should remove it. You want your neck and shoulders to show, don't you? Straps are so unsightly." Heather meant far more than Melanie's neck. She shook her head. If there was one rule, Melanie kept her mermaid outfit with her at all times. It was her mermaid tail and she never knew when she might be getting wet. But she could unbend a little. Her fish could accommodate any appearance, even that of clothing, hairpins and rings.

The real princess stood holding what Melanie would wear. Heather was right, it was plain by comparison to what Heather wore. But she was seeing the princess through the gown. The woman's charm, grace and character shaped it. A smile was more effective than any outfit. Everyone would forget the dress in the moment. Melanie could see that in Heather. Happiness came from within, and Heather was happy to be sharing.

Looking back at her reflection, Melanie examined herself. A swimsuit was nothing without the woman inside it. She would make the gown, not the other way around. Though a little magic wouldn't hurt. *Just don't outshine the princess...* There was no sense in not having fun, and Melanie loved being a mermaid. Some razzle-dazzle was in order.

To distract Heather, Melanie turned the talk back to the dress. "That's pretty."

"Try it on, then when you see that it's too 'yuck,' we'll go with the bubblegum pink." Heather then picked up her phone and checked her messages while Melanie slipped on the more than a little pretty sea-foam dress. "Wish I had another pearl necklace for you to wear, but mother dropped it to the bottom of the fish tank in the ballroom. The vicious fish won't let anyone near it." Heather spoke without looking up.

Speaking of fish, Melanie said to hers, "Do something with this." Melanie had in her mind a glittering wave in bright sunlight. She spun while her magic flowed from her, the swimsuit miraculously bending to both Heather's wishes and her own. They picked up Melanie's intentions from her mind and from Heather's, so Melanie wouldn't embarrass her. Heather would ignore Melanie if she was ugly in her eyes, and Melanie needed a girlfriend. Yet, she couldn't predict what the fish would do. They weren't hers to command completely. They had a mind and will of their own. And they were so much better at fulfilling what she wanted. Except this time.

The president's daughter's reaction was Melanie's first clue that she was in trouble. "What?" She turned to look in the floor length mirror. *I thought I told you 'Let hers be better.'*

They only do perfection, Ripple told her. He understood them far better than Melanie did. Since Ripple had become part of her mermaid clothing, he liked to look good, and this was so much better than good – and a complete disaster.

Melanie tried shifting the conversation again, but it was a weak attempt. "Do you have matching shoes?" How do you find shoes to match a living ocean wave? At least the fish had passed up on a tiara, though they'd thrown in a glittering necklace and earrings. Too much glitter, or not enough. She tried pulling up the sleeves to cover her shoulders, quite unsuccessfully.

"I should have worn that dress," Heather said on the way down the elevator. "They're all going to look at you. And such hair. I'm sorry. I'm jealous. It's not right of me, but I can't help it."

Melanie should have had her fish do the shoes too. These heels were killing her and she'd been on her feet since descending the elevator. The president's daughter returned to her friends and turned a shoulder on Melanie. She'd gotten the hint.

"May I?" asked a foreigner with a thick accent. Because Melanie hadn't learned how to say no, he was leading her towards the killing grounds, smiling, self-assured. All Melanie's self-confidence had been left upstairs. This guy was about to show Melanie that she hadn't danced yet. She tried to get him to be considerate, "My feet are killing me, be nice please."

"Not a chance." He flashed a smile then spun Melanie out and back. She was on her toes, his skill alone keeping her from falling. She blinked up at him, sure that she was about to forget her own name. He winked at her with a knowing smile. They knew one another, but Melanie didn't recognize him. Before she could place him, he spun her out again, giving her a taste of what was to come, and breathless they came together. "Don't let go," he forewarned her. Then it was one spin after another, until, well, Melanie lost sight of everything except his hands, brief glances of dark eyelashes and laughing eyes. He was having fun with Melanie and there was nothing she could do about it.

Finally, the music slowed. "I'm going to faint," Melanie said, though she was laughing, still on the balls of her feet. To drop her ankles were to break them if he got it in his mind to toss her again. She couldn't focus. The room was spinning. She'd forgotten every dance lesson she'd ever had. At some point, she became aware that they were walking. Her calves ached. Melanie thought her feet had gone numb, as there was no longer any pain. Their joined hands held high, they swayed through the casual waltz that came after the walk. Melanie followed his lead, glad that one of them could still think.

"You still don't know me?"

"How should I? I can barely see, and not straight. If you let go, I'm going to fall over."

"You're blind? I'm so sorry. I thought…"

Melanie laughed at him. "No silly, you've made me dizzy."

"It's the least I could do. You ruined my life. And thanks to you I gave up littering."

"What an odd thing to say. You sound almost mad at me for that."

"I am mad at you, but not for that. Well, ok, partially for that. You ditched me."

Attuning helped clear up his face, but not much more than that. Melanie was too done up for a thorough scan, and it wasn't like a simple ID system. She still had to use her brain.

And that right now was next to impossible. Her mouth only became dryer with the use of her powers. At least she was able to recover her sweat (and his, and that of those around them, gross as that was). Attuning was that gross. It gave everyone relief, but it didn't kick-start her brain into remembering him.

Melanie pretended to squint at his face, "I don't know you."

"I'm not that forgettable," he said.

Melanie laughed and used her hands to take away the hurt. Simple touch worked miracles. Maybe some time talking would restore her memory. "Can we get some water? I don't think my head is going to stop spinning."

"Sure. I don't suppose you've had a break all evening?"

He wasn't as adroit as her professor at arm-in-arm walking, but he was pleasant enough. Melanie liked him, even if she couldn't remember how she knew him. "No." Then she added, "You've been watching me."

"You're the prettiest girl here. Everybody else here is married, works here, or is trying to impress somebody. And you like dancing."

"Thanks. I think." Melanie took another opportunity to study his face. Dark eyes, eyebrows, eyelashes, curly dark hair, making it seem short. His face had a nice weathered look. If they knew one another, then he had to live on the sea, or at least spent a lot of time around water. Weathered hands too. They were oddly callused. That information didn't help. There was nothing about him that brought anything back to remembrance. Melanie met so many people, but that was no excuse. She felt really bad.

"Yeah, that probably didn't sound too flattering, did it?" he asked, misinterpreting her look.

"I'll take the 'prettiest' and toss out the rest, how's that?" Melanie smiled. "I'm sorry. I can't place you, but that shouldn't stop us from becoming friends. I'm Melanie…" But he didn't fall for her bait.

Stacy found her when they were waiting in line. "There you are. I've been looking all over." Melanie was so glad to see him. The name guessing was wearing on her. They couldn't seem to get past it. Maybe she could use Stacy's presence. An introduction where this guy would have to say his name…

"You had to only look on the dance floor. Dance masters have been throwing me about." Putting her arm in Stacy's, making it plain to her dance partner that she was leaving if he stayed recalcitrant, "Stacy this is…"

"Edvard. Edvard Channing, of the Daily Times. Nice to meet you Admiral O'Burk, sir."

Yes! Melanie wanted to high-five someone. *Edvard!* She repeated his name in her head, but nothing. This was so horrible. It reminded her of almost having her memory erased by sirens. Maybe she knew him from then. That might explain things. She hadn't thought she'd lost anything, but how would she know that she'd forgotten something? Unless someone like Edvard insisted he knew her and she didn't remember him.

"And you son. So, Melanie, you've promised me a dance," he smiled at her arm in his. It was a big old hint, but she was wilting, and not wanting to tell him no at the same time. Edvard came to her rescue.

"The lady needs a drink."

"Keep it to water, she's just a kid." Melanie aimed laser beams at Stacy for that. "Come find me," he said, ignoring her anger. He let her go, and then walked casually away. Melanie stared after him. He was being so nice.

"You're on first name basis with Admiral O'Burk?" Edvard asked after Stacy left, jerking her attention back around to him. "I don't think even his mother calls him Stacy."

Melanie laughed and snorted. "His mother calls him Admiral?" She again looked after Stacy, but he'd disappeared into the crowd. She laughed again, taking Edvard's arm. "Admiral, pick up your room." That was too much, and Melanie snorted again.

"Just so. He was born an admiral from what I've been told. What a fearsome child he must have been. So how come he lets you call him Stacy? I didn't even know he had a first name. And you dismissed him, out of hand, by the way. I don't think he minded."

"I didn't. He let me go, and he's my professor. I think Stacy is used to students treating him like that."

"Oh, thank you. Can I have two?" Melanie asked the blur that was the person serving drinks.

"I'm going to pour this first one over my head," Melanie said, when Edvard stepped them away from the press of bodies. "Food," the smell guided her feet, "This way…"

"Hold on," Edvard arrested her motion. "Drink one of those first."

"Oh, much better." Melanie was getting better at mimicking drinking, when in fact her body simply absorbed the water when she was dehydrated. Her upper lip sucked in that first glass, the water rushing right through her eyes to her brain, clearing her head. It wasn't nearly enough, but she was able to sip the next one at almost normal speed.

"You inhaled those. Want mine?"

"Desperately," Melanie looked sheepish as she polished off his as well, glad they were no longer talking about Stacy. The retired admiral turned professor, mermaid stalker and unusually polite gentleman tonight had her seriously confused. Edvard wasn't the guy to talk it out with. What Melanie needed was her girlfriends, and they were off cutting down Christmas trees. *Oh Jill, you're my best friend always, but you can be so stubborn.*

"You really do look ill. You must be famished. Come on," and Edvard took her arm, guiding her to the tables she'd visited earlier with Stacy. She never got a chance to actually eat any of it, including that huge brownie.

Her stomach rumbled at the thought of divine chocolate like that. Embarrassed, Melanie asked, "Don't you feel silly hanging out with a little girl?" Edvard was easily twice her age. And here she was dreaming of chocolate instead of his handsome profile. He really was a beautiful man. Kind when he wasn't withholding information.

"Now that you mention it," Edvard faked turned away. But they did get some distance between them. *So stupid Melanie!* "Just kidding. No. You trying to get rid of me?"

"Shouldn't you be off reporting, or something?"

"You are trying to get rid of me. But I'm not leaving yet. I'm hoping still for your story. And I am, I'm a freelancer. Though what I do and what I love are separate things, unfortunately. So, I fill the pages with droll trivial stuff. My editor pays for such stuff, but I'm more into real life stories." He gave Melanie a meaningful look.

"I don't read minds," Melanie said, hoping he didn't want a mermaid interview. She had his name now, but now she needed the where and how they met. "I'm tiring of the guessing game. You want me to remember. I won't make you tell me. I'm happy for the company. If Stacy hadn't grabbed me out, I'd be intimidated by all these important people."

Their conversation had hit a snag. Edvard wanted her to talk about something she'd threatened him about having to do with not polluting. Melanie was good with getting people to cooperate, when they wanted to anyway, and for the rest – she bashed heads. With those eyes and easy manner, Melanie would have been hard pressed either way.

Edvard broke into her thoughts, "You're welcome. Though I must ask, why are you here? If it's a state secret, wag your finger back and forth, like this, and I won't pry."

Melanie didn't give him the *that's a no-no* finger waggle. "I'm not sure I can say. How about a hint?"

"Hmm, Ok. The reason you're here. Does it have to do with how I found you sleeping in the river?"

"You mean in Denver? I wasn't sleeping, more like tied up. Or the Amazon, but I wasn't sleeping there either."

"Denver? You sleep with crocodiles?"

"I just said I wasn't."

"But you swam with them? Weren't you afraid?"

"Um, yeah, and no. I didn't think about it. The river was flooding and a friend and I helped the villagers clear the river." That was one of Melanie's favorite moments. Doing what a mermaid should, and for her that had been her first. Everything had clicked then. There was no going back.

"Wow. I don't suppose you can bring me in on your next adventure. You're so active."

Melanie rolled her eyes, "If you knew the half of it."

"So you're a Kung-Fu fighter then? Is that why you're light on your feet?"

"Now you're making me laugh. No. Nothing like that. But I think I got it now. I didn't used to sleep in water much." Melanie finally remembered the strange encounter. Exhausted from a day of cleaning the river, she'd worked late into the night and fallen asleep. Birds and fish had kept her company. He'd been kayaking in the early morning and had brought her breakfast. It was more than a coincidence, since he'd had two drinks, one unopened. "Did I ever thank you for the chai?"

"Your company is thanks enough."

Wow! "Make a girl blush, why don't you?"

"Seems like you're up for the challenge."

"Anyway. I'm sorry I forgot. That was years ago." It was Melanie's turn to be cagey.

"Years? That was only a few months ago."

"Hmm, well it seems like ages."

"Kids. No appreciation of time."

Melanie laughed right along with him. She'd gotten the response she wanted. He'd tortured her. "Yep, that's me. I'm sorry, it's insensitive for me not to have remembered."

"You know you're breaking my heart, right?"

Now what? Melanie wracked her mind. Oh right, the pollution thing. "Well, here I am."

"I was wanting more along the lines of the river girl I'd met."

"I'm that bad of a dancer? I knew it."

Edvard wouldn't let her derail the topic. "You said if I ever throw stuff into the river, I'd never see you again. Just so you know, I never have."

"You can't have been waiting for me to show up."

"I've thought of you every day since."

Well, hello wrecking ball. Now Melanie was speechless. She was going to cry in a second. Thinking of Jill, and now this.

Thankfully, Edvard was oblivious to her melting into a puddle. "Take a look at this," he said, bringing up his photos, displaying some beautiful pictures of a bunch of beautiful sea birds swimming in a copse of islands. "Flip through it."

Melanie shook her head, not daring to. She was already a mess. His saving that moment was going to destroy her. "Give me a second," she finally managed. Edvard slowly realized she was emotional and gave her some space to breathe. Blinking back tears, she took the phone.

"What am I supposed to see? Oh." Melanie's hand went to her mouth. "Has anyone else seen these?"

"No..." he stopped when Melanie squeezed him tight.

This was all wrong. Her emotions wanted what she couldn't have. *He's twice your age Melanie!* "You know we can't date, right?" As much as she hated admitting it, she said what Stacy had. "I'm just a kid. Though I'm older than I look." Mermaids, like fairies, lived a long time and stayed young looking.

“Can I at least get your phone number? We can at least text. An occasional call. And how much older? You look like my kid sister – fourteen or so.”

“Older, but not much to make up so big a difference.”

“You can stop calling me old.”

She laughed. *Sniff*, Melanie needed that. “Sorry. Here,” and Melanie shared her number. She wasn’t going to tell him to “talk to water,” but giving out her number seemed so much bigger. “I could use a big brother once and awhile.”

“You don’t have brothers?” Melanie shook her head, and the same to “Sisters?”

“Good friends though,” but a crease ran over Melanie’s face. She sighed. Jill stubbornness was a plague. She didn’t get that being a mermaid was the best thing ever and that experience should be shared. That moment in the jungle had been their best. It didn’t seem like they’d ever be mermaids together again, and it hurt so much. She was only concerned with mermaid lore instead of being one. If Jill simply lived as a mermaid did, she’d learn so much more.

“They can’t be that great of friends if they make you look like that.”

Melanie looked up shyly. Her troubles didn’t need to be his. “Best of friends, but we’re in a rough patch. It’ll blow over, I’m sure of it. At least, I really hope so.”

“How about a distraction?” At her nod, he turned her around. “Those fish in that fish tank are drawing a crowd.”

“What fish? I can’t see.” If her heart wasn’t in a thousand

pieces just then, she'd have reached out for them, or the water. Instead, he led the way through a bunch of people near the food tables. Melanie gasped when she saw the rather large fish tank. It was more than a dozen feet long, and tall. It was placed so as to give the caterers a place to work behind. A whole Christmas village was done up inside it, with electric Christmas lights and snowfall.

"How have I missed this?"

"Simply beautiful," Edvard said from beside her. "Too busy dancing. So why are all the fish on this side of the tank, do you suppose? What's in our direction that they want?"

The tank was pretty special, Melanie could see that. Edvard looked around and failed to see the obvious. They were looking at her. "Can we get closer?" There were so many people.

Heather spotted Melanie and pulled her into her group of friends. "I've never seen them act this way," she said.

"Isn't that's your mother's necklace?" one of Heather's friends asked.

"That's quite a toss," Edvard said, whispering into Melanie's ear. The necklace had landed around a tiny American flag in the center of the village. She remembered Heather mentioning it when Melanie was getting ready. At the time, Melanie had thought Heather might be making up the story. She was jealous of her, after all. Well, Melanie didn't hold that against her. They were talking again, so Melanie would do what she could to further that.

"We can get it," Melanie suggested. "While they're distracted." She could also use her influence. The fish would bring it up for her, if she asked. "Isn't that a ladder on the other side?"

"They probably use it for feeding the fish," Edvard said. "Good thinking. But we might get into trouble. It's not like we're ten anymore and it's expected we get into trouble. Though surely you can get it another time. It isn't going anywhere." Melanie frowned. She could help to retrieve it, to patch things up with Heather.

"No, I don't want to get it. It has to stay where it is," Heather said.

Melanie frowned, "Why not? If it's your mom's, wouldn't she appreciate it?"

"Because it's a magical necklace," Heather said in a hushed whisper, afraid someone might hear. Her friends tittered and then wandered off.

Edvard had the same reaction. Melanie could read it on his face. She'd seen it on so many others. His eyebrows shot up, *absurd*. "Magical? There's no such thing."

"Good, they left. You'd appreciate this Melanie, having ridden in on that deer outside." Edvard cocked his head at her, but refocused on Heather when she continued. "I used to think magic tales were for little kids, there being no substance to it. That is until Dad became president. There's too many unexplained 'miracles' happening around here. That necklace for one. Mom's health has dramatically improved since she's had it."

"Then why throw it in there if she's sick?" It didn't make any sense to Melanie.

"It's because it's a mermaid's necklace. As long as it's in sea water mixed with fresh…"

"Brine," Melanie finished for her. When Heather and Edvard looked at her, she continued, "The water where big rivers enter the sea is a mixture of sea and fresh waters. Certain fish live there and nowhere else. Too much salt water or fresh water, and they die. That kind of water is called 'brine.'"

"Yes, so the necklace in brine has special powers. You all know mermaid legends, right? That a mermaid can walk on land, except if she gets wet, she turns back into a mermaid. With that necklace on, a mermaid is immune to water's effects. It was a gift to mother. We'd like it to stay where it is."

"That stuff is pure fiction. There's no truth to it," Edvard said, taking Melanie's elbow and leading her away. "Right?" he asked Melanie when he'd gotten her far enough away from Heather.

"As far as I know," Melanie said. Except Ripple was another magical artifact, and intelligent too. He existed as part of her magical fish swimsuit. But Melanie didn't need him, not like that. The only other mermaid Melanie knew didn't either. Neither Jill or herself needed a magic trinket to have legs when wet. Until just then, Melanie had thought that that whole story was a story of popular fiction because it helped the whole plot. Had mermaids changed? Was Jill, and now Melanie, a new kind of mermaid? One that didn't need a magic trinket to have legs?

There might be truth to the legends, then. How horrible it would be to be a mermaid like that. To be afraid of water. Water was one of Melanie's best friends.

"What? You believe her."

Melanie shook her head and yawned. The dancing was catching up with her. "I'm not sure. It's all guesses."

"Before you fall asleep, you should find the admiral. Go fulfill your promise, before you turn into a pumpkin."

"I'm not about to turn into…"

"I'm teasing. Now go on. I've your number if you disappear on me."

"Thanks," but Melanie wasn't about to leave without a hug. She tried not to think about all the things he'd said while they hugged.

Trying not to think about them, though, was thinking about them. Before she could become beet red, she turned and dashed away off to interrupt Stacy, leaving Edvard to Heather's tender mercies. The woman had snuck up behind him, desiring one of his merciless dances.

7

Klutz

"You're tired?" Stacy asked, whisking her around in the waltz. Melanie was covering up a yawn. The party had been going on for hours, and yet it was just getting started for the majority of the president's friends. Probably because the president had yet to make an appearance. She wondered if he was going to want to dance too.

"Yes. Exhausted. But this is fun. Prom not so much. So, I'm soaking it up until, as Edvard says, I turn into a pumpkin." She shouldn't be tired. It was only eight or so at home, but Melanie was always up early. A swim and then out into the Rockies to find trees worthy of a home. Plus, she'd been on her feet all evening and hadn't eaten.

They finished that dance. Stacy was a very skilled dancer. Melanie really was enjoying herself. Stacy was more skilled than Edvard, Melanie thought. Grace defined him, whereas Edvard was flash. Melanie couldn't help comparing them. Who was the more skilled? And who did she like dancing with more? They were both fun, in their own ways.

Melanie finally settled on Stacy. He didn't make her dizzy, about to pass out and get sick on her shoes. That was a definite plus.

Near the end of that dance, there was a chill breeze and the sound of sleigh bells. "I've a surprise for you," Stacy said.

The crowed parted. Melanie thought it might be the president coming to claim a dance. He'd avoided her all night. And now when she was about to drop, he came. But if it was the president, then why did Stacy have the funniest expression ever?

Over the heads of everyone, Melanie saw tinsel and ribbons floating in thin air. What in the world? Then the crowd parted before her. It took Melanie a second to focus on the bedecked deer. Christmas ribbons flowed every which way and sweet tinkling silver bells sounded with every step and sway. The four female elves that he'd been entrusted to were so proud of themselves. Their smiles were so big, outshining Belfast's coat, which they had brushed into a brilliant sheen.

"You promised him a dance too," Stacy said, and gave Melanie a polite shove forward. The elves parted like geese and let her through. She touched his nose, trying to find the deer underneath his headdress.

"I feel like a neon sign," Belfast said by way of greetings.

"No. You look… Nice." Melanie told him. Her laughter matched his chagrin.

"I'm a circus clown."

Melanie didn't get a chance to tell him how cute he looked, because just then there was a squeak through the PA system. Everyone looked to the platform where the musicians sat.

"Ladies and gentleman, the president of the United States." Endless applause, and Melanie saw the president take the stage. When he spoke, he started by telling jokes, which got polite laughs. He went on, telling everyone about President Washington's escapade on Christmas Eve. It was fitting, Melanie thought. It was a rousing tribute to the first president, but then he surprised her.

"A toast!" Drinks were raised. A glass of something was pushed into her hands. It was so tempting to drink before the toast.

"Often we hear of the soldiers who laid down their life for our country. But we rarely hear of the women who sacrificed, and gave so that we might have our freedom. A friend of mine, descendant daughter of one of those women, is here tonight. She's helped to remind me of the gratitude we owe those many women. Some lost husbands, fathers, brothers and sons during the fight for our freedom, and others gave in so many other ways. It's what we're doing tonight, and every day – celebrating. All helped in ways that will never truly be known by the world so that we might live on in the land of the free. Tonight, let us remember them."

Melanie sniffed at the bouquet of the champagne she'd been given, taking her time to enjoy its fragrance. Taking a bit too long, Stacy was there to keep her from drinking it, replacing it with water. "One day," Melanie said.

"Yes, but not today," Stacy answered. "And besides, it isn't all that great."

He held up her phone. She'd given it to him before going off to change. "There are messages from your father. I've assured him you are safe, and being looked after. I'm not about to soil my reputation and let you drink this."

"But it's password protected."

"You entered your password a thousand times right in front of me at school. I remembered."

"I'm so changing it."

"Don't bother. I've programmed it to send me whatever new password you set."

"You can do that?"

Stacy laughed. "Well not me, but all the spooks that used to work for me can. So don't change it. I might need to let your father know you're ok."

"You have your own phone," Melanie said.

"True, but I like pretending I'm you. Your friends. The things they say."

"Give me that!"

"Nope. You have a dance to dance." Stacy laughed as he walked away, leaving Melanie fuming.

"What was that about?" Belfast asked. "I don't understand humans nearly so well as I'd like to. Seems he played you. You're much the same as the elvish women. An easy mark."

"Is that why you look like you got lost in a ribbon shop? We are that easy?" His smug nod got underneath Melanie's skin. "Are you going to heckle me, or be big and brave, wowing me with your dance skills?"

"Can't I do both?"

"Not if you're going to rub it in. Pouting women don't make great dance partners."

"I know. Look at that woman there. Her partner is miserable. The poor sap."

"That's Heather. The president's daughter." Melanie said. "I wonder what's gotten into her. She seemed fine earlier. Helped me with this dress. I really owe her."

"Are we going to dance, or talk? I've waited all night and endured those elves, all so I can dance with you."

"There it is. You were being nice for me. You really are a softie. Now, how do I dance with a deer?"

"Take my antlers. You've heard of the waltz? We deer invented it. We'll start with that. Then, if you can keep up, the swing after that." Melanie laughed. He couldn't be serious.

First thing Melanie missed was his guiding hands, but it turned out that antlers were just as good. The elves had fashioned the outer ones so she wouldn't prick her skin on their ends. After a bit, she wasn't sure she cared that he didn't have hands. He kept her entertained with elvish lore, describing the Winter Ball he was missing. "Everyone dances with deer. They know we're the best." There was a lot to be said for having a good dance partner, such as Stacy and Edvard, and the dozens that had preceded them, but she enjoyed her time with Belfast. And he was right. It seemed the waltz was made for four legs instead of two. Belfast spun her.

"Not so hard. I almost kicked those people in the face," Melanie said when she swung back. He didn't seem to care. He had a bit of Edvard in his style. For a time, people had let them dance alone, thinking Belfast "an animal." Melanie hoped that he'd prove them wrong, but after one round of applause she knew they only thought him well-trained. It was so sad for her. She didn't tell him any of it.

"Well, then I'll spin," Belfast said, not hearing the ache in her heart for people's carelessness. Melanie tried not to let it affect her, as she finally got a turn to get back at all the men that had kept her breathless all night. The marble floor and his hooves made for perfect spins. Those that had laughed at him were hanging from his sides. It was too funny not to laugh. Belfast was the perfect gent, standing still until they regained their feet.

"The perfect excuse for a breather," Belfast said. "I'm getting dizzy with all this spinning. I don't know how you girls do it. And so well too."

"Want to take a break?" Melanie asked. He shook his head; silver bells rang out. "No, no. I'm good for many more. Spin me the other way, and I bet my head clears up. Inside I'm spinning that way, so the other way should fix me right."

"Or you could focus on one thing as you go around, like me. Then you won't get dizzy."

"Is that your secret?"

"Give it a try," and she whirled him.

"Better, now you," and the two of them took turns, until unexpectedly out of nowhere, Melanie fell. Grabbing onto his antlers, the two of them spun, laughing. Carts of pastries whipped out of their way, caterers scrambling to save the food. Then the giant fish tank was suddenly near.

"We gotta stop!" Melanie cried, but there was no stopping them. Belfast slammed into the tank and she into him. It seemed like for one horrible moment that she'd caused a disaster. The water heaved and Melanie thought it might all go over. She told the fish she'd save them. But then nothing. The water sloshed back, maybe a little threatened to spill, but she put up a hand and it settled. "Whew," and they laughed at their narrow escape. The fish applauded and Melanie apologized for upsetting them. "That could have been so bad."

"Let's do it again!" Belfast begged.

Melanie looked at the chaos they'd caused. She shook her head. "If only we had the room to ourselves." There was Edvard nearby, watching, and she gave him a little wave. He had a pastry halfway to his mouth, stunned by their performance. The cad held the pose forever. Then he was shouting.

"Melanie!"

"What?" The fuss was over. No calamities today for Melanie. She hadn't broken anything. Well, except for the tray of stuff the elf server dropped when Melanie had said "elf." That was it. "There's no reason to panic, Edvard." But he couldn't hear her over the music and general conversation noise.

Edvard made dog-paddle waving motions. She stared at him. Was he choking? The sugar in those pastries would kill anyone, even if they were deliciously divine.

"Move!" he shouted, sounding desperate. Melanie finally understood he wasn't looking at her, but at what was behind her – the gigantic fish tank. But there was nothing to be afraid of, since water was her friend and so were the fish. If anything, she longed to dive in and turn into a mermaid. Wouldn't that shock all those dancers! Grab that necklace for Heather and her mom. The mermaid necklace might be helping her, but a real mermaid was infinitely better. If only she was so bold.

She turned about, and a wall of blue was before her nose. The tank slid off its support, kicking out the cart it sat upon. The thousand-gallon fish tank came crashing down at her feet, exploding everywhere, Melanie getting the brunt of it. Not even Ripple was fast enough to do anything to help her. Water was doing its best to not harm her, but she was drenched, the Christmas village knocking her off her feet. She almost laughed, but she hurt all over, and the wave that swept across the dance floor needed her guidance. But it was so difficult in the dress. Melanie had enough strength to save only a few, so she decided to keep the wave away from an elderly couple. The rest went down under the wave. And for that, she blacked out for a second.

When she could see again, people were picking themselves up. Edvard was on his knees, Stacy holding his arm, steadying him. It seemed fitting that the admiral would have kept his feet. Somehow, Melanie hadn't died right then.

Belfast lapped at the water. His narrow legs had kept him above the raging current.

"Don't lick that!" Melanie told Belfast. "There's glass."

Again, Melanie had brought disaster. Trouble seemed to always followed her no matter how hard she tried. She just didn't think dancing with a deer in a ballroom was certain to end in a disaster. Belfast had been so eager to prove himself.

Stacy joined her first, seeing her expression, "Don't blame yourself. Bringing a deer in here was as much my fault as yours, or anyone's."

"You didn't dance with him." Stacy shrugged. If she wanted to blame herself, he was done trying to get her to stop.

Edvard hustled in, slipping and sliding. "You should get off the floor too." He reached to help her up.

"Careful of the fish," Melanie said.

"Yeah, where are they?" Edvard looked around, being careful where he stepped. Taking Melanie's hands, he snatched them back. "Ow! Something bit me."

"I warned you."

"Ouch, I'm bleeding." He sucked at his hand. "Ugh, that water tastes horrible."

"Anyone hurt?" The able bodied among the tuxes arrived.

"Just my pride," Melanie said, though she hurt worse than a fall. The glass had cut her, but she tried not to let it show. All the magic she had left she used to keep the blood off the dress. Heather would kill her if she ruined it.

"The fish bit me," Edvard said, pointing to the rows and rows of fish on Melanie's arms. President MacLeod arrived on that note, his daughter and wife on his arms. They all took in the fish lined up like chessmen on Melanie's arms. Up her shoulders and down her legs were everything living that had lived in the fish tank.

"You look like a mermaid," Heather said. There were several gasps, the elves all looking at her with round eyes. "Well, she does." Then everyone laughed. Melanie too, eventually. It was funny if you didn't believe in mermaids.

"You ok?" President MacLeod asked, squatting down beside Melanie, pulling broken village houses away.

Melanie shook her head, "I'm sitting on about every hard edge that was in that thing."

"There's blood back here," he whispered so only those that were close could hear. Slowly he drew away more things.

"Hold on. Someone get the doctor."

"I'm ok," Melanie said. "Really."

"You have dozens of cuts," Edvard said squatting on the other side of her, helping the president get her out of the Christmas village, "so you're probably in shock."

"Let's get her up," President MacLeod ordered. "Get the cart that held the tank. We'll put her on it."

"Careful of the fish," Melanie warned again.

"She means it," Edvard said, being careful as he took her elbow and shoulder. "They bite."

"On three," the president said. With so many to help, Melanie was hoisted and set on the cart without fuss.

"Mother's necklace!" Heather jumped in where Melanie had sat.

"So that's what I sat on," and everyone laughed at her humor. They looked so serious. She must be in some kind of shock not to be feeling it.

"And about every shard of glass. You should be in ribbons," Edvard said.

"Water's my friend," Melanie said.

"Yeah, but," Edvard said looking at the glittering pile of glass. "It doesn't make any sense."

"Keep the conversation positive," Stacy said. They wanted her to think good thoughts and not dwell on what could possibly be wrong. It can't be that bad.

"I'm fine," Melanie grunted. A flash of pain at her feet and she saw Stacy squeezing one of her toes. He wagged his finger at her. "Hush," he mouthed.

"To the residence," the president said.

The doctor arrived when they reached the elevator. "My office would be better," the doctor said. Then he took one look at the rows of hungry fish and threw up his hands.

"We need to settle them first, right Melanie?" the president said. He seemed to be taking it better than anyone.

"Yes, please."

"There's another fish tank in my study." He jerked his head, meaning up the elevator. "Stacy, as her confidant, may come. Young man, please wait here."

"Call me in a couple days," Melanie said to Edvard as they wheeled her into the elevator. He nodded and then the door closed on Melanie with the president, his wife, Heather, the doctor and Stacy.

"I'm sorry everyone," Melanie said. "I ruined your party."

"Hold on Melanie," the president's wife said. "Call me Julia. I'm here with you through everything." She wanted to take Melanie's hand, so the fish moved aside, inching closer to one another. In a minute they arrived in a palatial setting. Priceless art decorated the hall and Melanie wanted to see it all, but there were too many people with her for her to catch more than a glimpse of each. Then they wheeled Melanie into a cozy library. A fire burned in the fireplace. In the corner, a perfectly decorated Christmas tree sparkled, underneath it a heaping pile of presents were all beautifully wrapped. On them, Melanie saw the same ribbons the elves had adorned Belfast with.

"Belfast should be here. Is someone looking after him?"

"Oh, I forgot it was being cleaned," President MacLeod said, distracting Melanie. They all looked at the empty tank.

"Water," Melanie barked. "I can make more brine, but I'll need water."

"She's delirious," the doctor said.

"Do as she says," Stacy countered.

President MacLeod looked at Stacy, then to the doctor and finally to Melanie and gave a nod. He recognized that Melanie was saying it by what she was, not just on some whim. He'd seen her move water before. "Ok then. Everyone out except Stacy."

"Julia please stay. Heather too. I'm going to need to change," she said.

"How much water do you need?"

"Enough to fill that," Melanie said, pointing at the tank. "Ladies, please. Remove the dress."

"Stacy and I are going for water." The guys beat a hasty retreat while the girls helped Melanie.

"What's happening?" Heather asked her mother, talking over Melanie.

Julia shrugged, "This must be one of those times we don't talk about. So, young lady, why are you ordering my husband around?"

"I'm not. I just asked for water."

"Demanded, more like," Heather said.

"She decent?" MacLeod called in after a few minutes.

"Yes, we're almost done. She's wearing a swimsuit anyway," Heather said. "I guess it's a good thing you kept it."

"I never know when I'm going to get wet," Melanie said in all seriousness. Though seeing the blood red dress, Melanie felt ill. What was the matter with her? Why couldn't she feel anything? The talking helped to distract her.

"Does it happen often?"

"All the time," Melanie smiled. The dress gone, Melanie called Stacy over. "I need a back rest." He looked at her strangely, but came to support her. "And put me over by the tank."

"Now the water." MacLeod lifted an ice bucket from their upstairs kitchen. "Pour it on me." His eyebrows rose, but he did as she said. Relief poured into her. "Better," Melanie said. "You might want to move," she told him. "I'm about to change." The fish of her suit were racing over her legs. It would be a little slower than normal, but it was still rather fast. The president had about a second before a large fin passed where he'd been standing. "Oh that hurts," Melanie fell back against Stacy.

"Oh my gosh," Heather stood there, unable to believe her eyes.

"She's not well," the First Lady said, putting her hand to Melanie's forehead.

The Christmas tree in the corner began to shake. A rushing wind sound presaged, the wind chimes followed with a whirling glow. Gravity ceased and they started to float.

"Ri'Anne stop it," Melanie blurted.

In a blink, there was a five-inch girl fluttering over her chest. The girl pointed a finger and they all had weight again. “You were about to fall. Do you know what that’s like when you lose your best friend?”

“Yes, because you tell me every time you rescue me.”

“Well, in my futures, you were really hurt. *Are* really hurt, oh my gosh!” With a blink she was gone, and out in the hall Melanie heard the doctor cry out, “Hey!” In stumbled the doctor, with Ri’Anne like a wasp shoving, pushing, pulling, glowing brighter than the angel on top of the Christmas tree. The man stumbled upon Melanie’s cart. “Treat her, now!”

“Ri’Anne, I have… to… get… the fish into the tank, first.” One by one, faster than Melanie could say it, the fish disappeared off her arms and legs. Ri’Anne grabbed every bit of flotsam and tossed them in the empty fish tank. Melanie cried out. It had been the fish keeping her painless.

“What’s the matter with you?” Ri’Anne hummed over her face. Melanie not able to focus. It felt like she was dreaming. “You have to tell me. In this future or any other.” She crossed back and forth. Then Ri’Anne turned on the others. “What were you doing? Why is she like this?”

Before anyone could answer, Ri’Anne started barking orders. In some future, they’d answered her, and so she used that information now instead of waiting. It could be quite infuriating. She was carrying on both sides of a conversation, and Melanie did not get to speak. To keep Melanie from getting mad at her, Ri’Anne had had to learn to let Melanie have her say. Though when Ri’Anne was agitated, it all went out the window, as was happening now.

Melanie could only hope Ri’Anne would be fast enough.

"Help me," Ri'Anne was in the president's face. "Hold her hand over the tank. No, don't worry. She's awake, but we must hurry." Then she hovered in front of Julia. The First Lady's eyes crossed to try and focus on Ri'Anne. "This other hand in the water." Julia nodded that she understood.

"Heather, the water," Julia said.

"Professor, hold her up." Ri'Anne fluttered her transparent, translucent and glimmering wings at the man. "She's slipping. The fish are in the tank and can no longer bite you."

When the people didn't move fast enough, Ri'Anne became her regular size, flying up and over Melanie's cart, flying out of the room with an empty pail and back again before she'd really left. The water flowed into Melanie's right hand, up her arm and down her side to the tips of her flipper, then back up and out her left. In the journey, the tap water became the kind these fish enjoyed.

Throughout the process, Ri'Anne kept up a diatribe with the doctor, tossing things out of his bag and coming up with bandages and scissors before he could ask for them, placing them in his hands. She was being the light he needed.

"You, my lady, are really hurt," the doctor said to Melanie as he worked. "You should be in a hospital, not doing this."

"The Island might be able to help," a tiny finger poked Melanie on her dimpled chin. But Melanie shook her head slightly.

"You'd think I'd get used to this," Stacy said, meeting the president's eyes. "But Melanie is, well… Everybody knows she's the prettiest girl. I just had no idea. I mean, I knew she was different, imperious, impertinent, demanding and a woman of unmeasured love and compassion. Is this why?"

"No," Ri'Anne fluttered up in front of her professor. "She's always been this way. Though the imperious, demanding parts, those are new." She looked down at her friend with a smile. "She can hear us. We're almost finished."

Melanie went limp as the last drop of the brine left her. Whatever strength she'd had left vaporized. Ri'Anne's voice snuggled up close and comforted Melanie as she slipped away.

8

Imperious

"Who's Edvard?" Ri'Anne asked, sitting crosslegged before Melanie's eyes as she awoke.

She'd probably just sat down, knowing when Melanie would awake. But without knowing for sure, Melanie was terribly warmed to see her friend first thing. And she looked cute too. All part of being a fairy. It made sense, because Melanie felt like a giant cat, seeing her friend so small. A quick inhale and she could have her friend for breakfast.

"Don't you dare, Melanie McKenzie. You're supposed to rest."

There it was, Ri'Anne knowing what Melanie had been thinking. Because in some future, Melanie had actually done as she'd thought. It was still tempting, anyway. Fairies were really light, like dragonflies, able to walk on leaves. She could really breathe in her friend if she wanted to, but gave up the thought. It wouldn't be worth riling up her friend.

Lying on her stomach, her chin resting on her folded arms, she turned her thoughts back to what Ri'Anne had asked. *Ed-*

vard? Edvard was the really cute and aggravating guy that had danced her feet off.

"Oh, he's nice. I like him," Ri'Anne said before Melanie said anything. Melanie just sighed. A hard part of being Ri'Anne's friend was that Melanie liked talking too, and unless she said something, Ri'Anne wouldn't know. At the moment, though, Melanie didn't care enough to make an issue of it.

Then Ri'Anne ticked points off her fingers, "I'm to tell you to rest, and I'd answer all your questions before you say them, but that would just get you mad and upset. And I've promised the doctor not to do that. So, ask. I know you want to talk about two days ago. And yes, it's been two days and it's Christmas Eve." There she went again, carrying on the conversation. In her head, Melanie supposed it was difficult to separate the future from the moment. It was kind of funny, but Melanie didn't laugh because Ri'Anne would ask what was funny, and Melanie wouldn't say. Ah, and here Melanie was carrying on a conversation all on her own. She shouldn't hold it against her friend as well.

Ri'Anne stood and paced, then she crossed her legs at the knees, toes pointed inward, fingers on her chin, waiting on Melanie to say something, Melanie hadn't a clue what. What had she been thinking about? Oh right! The conversation from when she'd conked out.

"I'm not imperious!" Melanie said.

Ri'Anne mentally counted to five (at human speed), which was an insufferable eternity for a fairy. "Yes you are. It bothers you that we see it."

"I'm not imperious," Melanie said, hurt.

"The very fact you have to defend yourself on the matter

gives weight to the argument against you."

"But I'm not."

"When you're full of your Sea Lord authority, you bellow."

"I don't bellow!" Melanie countered.

"Maybe it's billow."

"I thought you weren't supposed to get me upset. It's not working."

"It's true," Ri'Anne said, sinking back into a cross-legged position. "Then you have to stop being so imperious. Besides, nobody said you were obnoxious about it."

"Well, thanks," Melanie said, pretty sure that Ri'Anne wasn't complementing her. But now she looked too cute to argue with anymore.

"You're welcome," Ri'Anne said, bouncing to her feet and leaning in to hug Melanie, wrapping herself around her nose. Her fluttering wings batted against Melanie's eyes and cheeks. Melanie's heart melted.

"You worry me," Ri'Anne said after a while. "Look at you. Laid up and stuff, because you gave your all to save a bunch of fish. We're in the White House for crying out loud. There's a dozen Christmas parties to attend. We should be having fun. Instead I'm up here playing nurse."

Melanie knew Ri'Anne wouldn't join in the festivities without a friend. She was right where she wanted to be. Making friends wasn't her best trait, so she held onto those she had. If she went to the party, she wouldn't mingle as easily as Melanie would.

"And Stacy?" Melanie asked.

Ri'Anne sat back down, "Our professor is hereabouts, somewhere. He promised to stick around until you recovered."

"How's Belfast?"

"Oh, he's got the elves adorning him with ribbons last I looked. You know there are elves here?"

"Yes, I saw. Though I didn't know you knew about them."

Tossing her hands, Ri'Anne nodded. "I'm a little nervous around them. As one of fairy-kind, I'm rather new on the block."

"You're not normally shy. Charge in there, anticipate their questions and be a bugger for about five seconds, then the ice will be broken."

"It's not as fun with them. They don't have spikey thoughts like everyone else. I think it's because they think ahead more on what they want to say, and don't say what they were thinking."

"You mean they think before they talk, like our parents taught us to do but we don't."

"It's more than that. We're varied. Possibilities abound. Maybe it's because we don't know what we want, or we're still trying to figure out how to get where we want to go. With our lives, that is."

"And the elves are more settled?"

"Yeah, so that's why I'm intimidated."

"You cry over falling leaves," Melanie countered.

"Hey, I'm being nice here. You should hear the trees at the change of the season. You'd cry too."

"I'm sure spring will be nice. You'll love it, I'm sure."

"Want to fill me in on Edvard," Ri'Anne changed the subject. She'd probably been thinking about him non-stop. Melanie had avoided thinking of wonder boy. Truth was, Melanie was mixed up. Edvard was infuriating, caring and dashing, all in one. It was a potent combo. If he wasn't twice her age, she'd love nothing better than to try and sort him out.

Since Melanie wasn't talking, Ri'Anne picked her thoughts out of the cosmos where she was chatty. "Ah, good. You need a crush. Too bad he's older. I've kept in touch with texts. Stacy gave me your phone. He wanted a picture…"

"You didn't!?"

"Yep, and of your sleeping face. Don't be such a worry wart. I brushed your hair and pushed your lips into a smile."

"Um thanks," Melanie said, but Ri'Anne had disappeared, and then was back a minute later, shoving a shirt at her.

"Put this on. You're all better, and we're about to have company." She then disappeared when Melanie sat up. Then reappeared behind her in normal size and helped Melanie on with the shirt and then brushed out her hair.

"I'm better?" Melanie did feel good. Really good. And in the motion of letting her hands down, her fingers touched a necklace. She knew instantly the reason she felt better was because she wore the mermaid necklace. It had helped her. But what about Julia? The First Lady needed it too. "No," Melanie started to say.

Ri'Anne touched her lips, silencing Melanie. "Say it with him." She nodded to the door, where someone knocked at that exact moment. Ri'Anne flew over, landed and waited for Melanie's thoughts to catch up. Ri'Anne gave her a whole second, then opened the door.

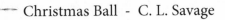

"Anticipating me again Ri'Anne? However do you do it?" President MacLeod asked.

"Come on in," Ri'Anne said with a bow. "Melanie's waiting and resting, as ordered." Ri'Anne was way and above on her best behavior. It sparked Melanie's curiosity, but without being able to see into the future like Ri'Anne, she had to wait for events to unfold naturally.

"Call me Tolvar," the president said. "Between us, your kind and mine, I think we should be on first names. I've been thinking about this. My life is complicated enough as it is. Maybe someday we'll be more official. Do ambassadors and things if life merits it. Until then, I want us to be friends."

Melanie saw Ri'Anne think about that. What should she say? In the end, she looked to Melanie. She wanted her help. Future relations between fairies and humans, mermaids and all things magical. But Melanie wanted Ri'Anne to answer for herself.

"I'm ok with being friends personally. The official side of things is built on trust, though. With the way your government treated Melanie, I've had a hard time with that. You hurt me a lot."

The President said, "Stacy explained. I'm sorry."

"Ri'Anne takes hurt against me personally."

"I can't lose her," and Melanie was suddenly in a bear hug. Ri'Anne held her tight, proving that Melanie really was recovered. "She's the only one that believes in me."

"It's good to have friends," Tolvar said, scooting an upholstered chair to the bed and sitting down. He twined his hands, and Melanie saw shadows under his eyes. He hadn't been having fun. The parties Ri'Anne mentioned were going on without him. Was this why Ri'Anne acted strangely? What global catastrophe had him up all night? Instead of breaking under whatever had him down, he focused on Melanie. "How are you feeling?"

"I'm good," Melanie said. "Thanks." She would get up if she wasn't in a shirt and swimsuit. Around a pool she'd be fine, but the president was in a suit and this was his house, even if he did want to call them friends. "The necklace healed me. How's your wife?"

Tolvar looked down at his hands at the question. Ri'Anne got up and paced to the door, her back to it, hand on the handle. What did she know of what was about to be said? Melanie looked at the president. He was crying.

"This is where she gets imperious," Ri'Anne dropped.

"We said our goodbyes, she wanted me to leave the hospital. She didn't want the fuss."

"What do you mean? Hospital? Goodbyes? She's dying?" At his silent nod, Melanie jumped up. "That's not going to happen. Ri'Anne, get them," then she knelt beside the president. "We're going to the hospital. Come with us." Ri'Anne came back in followed by two of his agents. She shut the door.

"Of course, I'll come. I shouldn't have left. But she wanted me to see you."

"Ripple?" Melanie called to the magic portal that made its home in her swimsuit.

A magic wave flowed from Melanie, drifted over to the wall and a window to a hospital room appeared. There, Melanie saw Julia lying pale, and Heather beside her.

"What's this?" President MacLeod said. He looked from it and back to Melanie, then to Ri'Anne, then to his agents, and asked, "You're elves?"

They heaved a sigh. "We're so fired."

"Nobody's getting fired. But it makes sense that you'd get the elves off my detail when you showed off this," President MacLeod said.

"Take my hand," Melanie told him and lifted him out of his chair.

"The doctor, is he an elf too?"

Ri'Anne shook her head no. "I was desperate, and he'll keep our secret. Though he wants Melanie to give his granddaughters mermaid swims." The elves laughed at this.

"I want a mermaid swim," Tolvar said, but knew that was impossible as long as he was president. His duties as president gave him very little free time. "Some other time."

They were about to step into the portal. Heather by then had noticed the shimmer, as it was seen on the other side. In that pool she saw her father, not quite understanding what was happening. Understandable, Melanie thought. She stepped through and pulled the president through behind her, Ri'Anne and the others following.

Heather gasped and then ran, sobbing into her father's arms. Other than her, there were only the beeps from the medical equipment. Melanie went to the First Lady and touched her forehead, releasing water from her fingertips. They'd kept Melanie hydrated while she recovered. Using the water connection, Melanie looked around in the woman. The water within her was sick with disease. Melanie had seen something like this before. Jill had brought her and her friends to an ill river, but this was in a person. Melanie felt Ri'Anne's touch. Her friend's bright light backed her up, comforting her. *Why?* Melanie reached out wider.

Melanie gasped. The same disease that was killing the first lady was in the president and first daughter as well. The elves were fine, and so was she and Ri'Anne.

"Ri'Anne..." and she was gone. **Get the doctor, the nurses I need to test them... Those you know to be infected. And get me water.** There were times when Ri'Anne's foreknowledge was super helpful.

Melanie went to the sink, turned it on and stopped the drains. Though not really necessary, she did it out of habit. She called to the water inside herself, which was calling to the water in each room where Ri'Anne had turned on the faucets. The water went for the First Lady, then it began trickling in from the closest rooms.

The agents outside the room came in, looked around and in shock asked, "Sir, how did you get here?" The doctor rushed in before Tolvar could reply.

"What's going on here?" He was looking at the tiny stream running between his feet.

"The president's been infected, and so is Heather. I'm filling the room with water. We're going for a swim." Everybody just looked at Melanie, with that mouth agape expression she'd come to expect when she did anything majorly unexpected.

"How's that supposed to help?" the doctor asked.

"Stay and see," Ri'Anne said, returning. "I've turned on all the faucets on this floor."

Melanie closed her eyes and called to the water, "Come quickly." She had visions of patients in some rooms wondering about their faucets spontaneously coming on, and sinks filling up to overflowing. At Melanie's beckoning, the patients watched their puddles run out and join to others in the hall, the whole of it running towards the private wing where they were.

At the sound of rushing water, the doctor turned about. He saw nurses all down the hallway clutching clipboards and jumping up onto furniture. Waves battered aside doors. They gained in in size as they came.

"We have a pool!" The doctor turned on Ri'Anne, thinking her the culprit. He should have known better. The first wave crashed around him. "And you could have turned on the hot water as well. It's freezing." The next wave to enter was warmer. Ri'Anne anticipated him.

"Moving her might be dangerous," Ri'Anne said, floating over the rising water. "C'mon in," she told the three nurses she'd gathered. The two women and one man looked at the knee-high water and waves rolling in. The waves weren't nearly as big as the first couple. "You're infected. You need this."

"They're infected?" the doctor shouted in alarm. "This room should be quarantined!"

"They are the only ones infected, doctor," Ri'Anne said. "I know, just as I know you had two jelly donuts instead of the ham sandwich your wife packed for you for lunch. Now please sit. You need what Melanie's about to do, too. The rest of you can leave," she told the agents that had come in. The elves shook their head, said they'd stay. Then Ri'Anne left too. She wasn't much for water, if she could help it. Before the room flowed over, she went to shut off the faucets.

Everyone was swimming, thinking they had to keep their heads up. It was only Melanie and the First Lady underwater. "Come on down," Melanie told them. "It's no use fighting it. The room will be full in a few more seconds." And then it was. "Breathe normally," Melanie coached them.

"I told you, water is my friend," Melanie told the president when he dropped down beside her, grasping the bed. Reaching out, he drew Heather to him. The two looked at Melanie and then to Julia. She appeared to be sleeping.

"How's she doing?"

"Better. The water is having an effect." Though it was more than the water.

What was needed was someone that made water their friend. The water flowed into her, like she'd done for the fish that needed brine water, and came out changed, replaced by still more water, gathering in potency as she channeled it.

The elvish secret service agents helped the nurses down to the floor and then set out swimming, mostly to stay out of the way. It was obvious they were enjoying what Melanie was doing. Their joy was infectious.

"I've wanted to do this, for like ever." The woman swam about, "I'm a bird..."

"Me too," said the other elf. "C'mon Mr. President. She'll wake up in a second. You'll see."

When the moment was right, Melanie gathered the water and burst it forth. Everyone held on as waves pounded in and through them. The black spots like mini tadpoles broke apart within the bodies of the diseased. Though with each pulse, the water dwindled. Melanie was quickly running out of water, and there was still more to do. The president and his daughter were cleansed, as were the nurses. But Julia had more of the disease than the others and internal damage as well. She had a second before the water dried up and she'd be powerless. What Melanie needed was true water, not filtered faucet water, but a living breathing source. The sea was too far, but maybe the Potomac was near enough. It would have to be. But she couldn't take everyone.

Ri'Anne, find us at the river, and then Melanie took the president, his wife, daughter and elves through. Over their heads a large boat passed, its propeller churning the water. The president held to his wife, wrapping her in Heather's coat. They floated amid the river. The murky bottom vaguely below them.

"Wow, so this is what that's like," Tolvar said. "My vision of General Washington included an underwater trip. I'm really in awe, but why are we here?"

"I'm sorry," Melanie told them. "I needed more water and its power. Natural rivers have strength that filtered water lacks." And it lived. The river gave her what she needed, and with only one patient, she gave it all to the first lady. The president was the first to notice her wake. Julia's eyes fluttered in surprise at the circumstances.

Melanie called to her friend, **Belfast, need a ride. Bring the elves.**

Ri'Anne joined them, shining into the river, giving them what light she could.

"We're done here. C'mon," Melanie said, swimming beside the president and Julia. The two of them were enjoying themselves. They headed for the river bank.

Before they got there, Melanie sensed a crowded shore. Several girls dove in and swam down to her. Cleo dive bombed her and wrapped her arms about Melanie's neck. "What? How?"

"We've missed you," Cleo said. Lucy and Jill joined them. "Ri'Anne, of course."

"As I have you," Melanie hugged each of her friends. "And I'm sorry," she told Jill. "Your friendship means more to me, than about anything, except this. I don't want to lose you." It was tearing Melanie apart, but getting the words out felt good.

"No, it's me," Jill said. "I love you. You know I do. But all of this? I just can't. If Cleo hadn't dragged me..." And there they were at the same old impasse, the barrier that separated them staring at them in the face.

"Excuse me… Hi," Heather said, holding her mother's hand. The president looked on with elves peeking over his head. "What's happening?"

"My friends were making up," Cleo said. "But now I'm not so sure. They can sure make a fuss over nothing. They're mermaids, if you didn't know. I am too, but I must want it. Sorry I'm not making sense. What were you asking?"

"Can we say thank you and go home?" President MacLeod said.

"Yes. One second," and Cleo turned, tapping Melanie on the shoulder. They chatted for a minute and Cleo returned. "Melanie says the Washington Monument is right over there. Ri'Anne had your people come. They are on shore waiting for you. Melanie will be right with you and will dry you off."

Tolvar looked upset that he didn't get to say the goodbye he wanted to Melanie. Once out of the water, he'd have to return to being the president. But he turned and made the journey. But Melanie was there before he surfaced. "Thanks," she said.

"And you," Tolvar said, taking her hands, "for everything." His ladies squeezed in close. "If there's ever anything…"

"An invitation to the next Christmas ball?"

"Done," Julia said.

"We'll send the dress," Tolvar said. "But to where?"

"Ask Stacy," Melanie said.

"Can I hug you?" Melanie asked, looking to the elves. They were, after all, Secret Service agents. They nodded enthusiastically. Tolvar took Melanie in his arms and they hugged. Then they were drifting apart.

It was the most difficult parting Tolvar had experienced in his years in the White House. But from the bottom of the Potomac, it was the most surprising. What better way to spend Christmas? In his hands were his two loves, and the view was breathtaking. With a last look around and a nod to the girl who had changed his life, he turned. Striding from the river, cameras picked up the three of them, their lights blinding for a moment. The press pool was full of questions, asking about the turn of events that had brought them to the river. He thought about it and said, "Our nation has many remedies for the ailments that we've yet to tap. Our waterways have served our country for many years. I think we've forgotten how fundamental they are to our strength. As you can see, my wife Julia has been brought back from the brink of death. This will be taken as a victory, of many more to come. Let's celebrate. Merry Christmas everyone."

Tolvar had managed to capture the attention of everyone,

so few noticed the girls that had come from the river. His clothes were dry as promised, but he was still cold. Snow was falling again, and he was concerned for Julia. Heather's coat hid the hospital gown, but she'd be cold. But she'd hung back to thank the sea maid herself. Heather had kept the president company during his short address. Julia soon joined her husband and daughter, thankful for the events that had given her more time with them.

"Sir, the paper you requested," an agent said, handing Tolvar a note.

But I didn't. Then Tolvar opened it up and read, "Heather, it's for," and he nodded towards the river. He wanted to take it himself, though. There had to be a better excuse than next year's Christmas ball to call on the girl. He laughed to himself, even if she did drown his parties, it had been worth it. Christmas of next year couldn't come soon enough. Then, when he got out of office he was going to make a special trip to Boulder, Colorado and find out why mermaids chose that location to live.

Walking behind the presidential party, Melanie was quiet, her thoughts echoing the president's. Belfast, along with a pair of elves, followed Melanie and her friends. "I can't believe they're elves," Cleo said, looking at the two. "They look like everyone else."

"There's more magic people like them," Ri'Anne said, having returned to her full-sized self. "After this, I bet we'll begin to see more of them."

"To what end?" Lucy asked. "There will be problems. The world is difficult enough as it is."

"Well, there will be more magic," Cleo said, eyes wide. "C'mon. We're in Washington, DC. And there's the Washington Monument. This is exciting."

Stacy and Heather each joined the group of women from opposite directions.

"For you," Heather said, stuffing a paper in Melanie's hands. Then Heather hugged her, holding on forever, and then said, stepping back, "I'm sorry. I was so jealous. You were dancing with everyone. I tripped you. It's my fault for everything, for the fish tank breaking. I'm so sorry." She then turned and fled.

"You went to a ball?!" Cleo grabbed Melanie's arms. "I want to hear everything!" Ri'Anne was right behind her. She hadn't known Melanie had been dancing.

Stacy spoke to nobody in particular. "I'm stuck in meetings, and you go swimming with the president. That's got to be a first. A president swimming with mermaids."

"Not so, Stacy," and Melanie handed him the paper.

"What's this?" Stacy read.

"Stacy?" Cleo, Jill and Lucy asked at the same time.

"This is amazing. George Washington. I recognize the handwriting. But who's Myrtle?"

Jill snatched the paper out of his hands nearly as fast as fairy might and read through it quickly. "You knew this?" she turned on Melanie, mixed fury and surprise in her expression.

"I read it when I arrived here. I thought you might want that, with all your research into our past." Melanie didn't finish getting the words out before Jill threw her arms around her neck in a fierce hug, holding tight for several seconds. Then

Jill let go, and poof was gone, taking the paper with her.

"What was that all about?" Melanie asked, confused. Everyone looked at her. If Melanie didn't know, then nobody did.

"For a mermaid that doesn't like to display her powers, that was a pretty amazing display," Lucy said.

"The snow mostly obscured things, and nobody was paying them any attention," Ri'Anne said.

"I was going to ask how you were planning on getting home," Stacy said. But with a swirl of his fingers, he thought a mermaid ride might be the way to go. The same as Jill.

"Want a ride?" Melanie asked.

"Military flights are cheap, but… You're not coming, are you?"

"I have to take Belfast home, but I can send you all to Boulder."

"Meet us at Jill's. Everyone will be waiting to do the gift exchange," Ri'Anne said and gave her a hug.

"I'll try not to be too long," Melanie said.

"No more adventures!" Cleo ordered. She quickly hugged Melanie, then stepped back as snow starting swirling about.

"I can't promise anything." Unlike Jill, she didn't let stray bystanders get a view of them. She brought in the snow, then when nobody could see anything, sent her friends home. Dropping back, she stood beside Belfast. The elves that had been walking him gave her a hug and then hurried after their friends, disappearing into the little storm Melanie had created.

"Come along Belfast," and Melanie climbed up on him. She picked up his reins as they trotted north, taking a few passages he suggested. She stopped them overlooking a snowfield in northern Canada before drifting into the tundra of the far north. Reaching icy plains, Melanie looked at ice and snow in every direction. "Wow it's cold here."

"This is far enough," Belfast said. Elves popped out of the snow to help Melanie dismount and remove the halter from Belfast. "Someday it'd be great if you visited, but I know your friends are waiting for you. I'll miss you."

"I'll miss you too," Melanie hugged him, then hopped down. When she released the reins, Melanie lost sight of the elves and Belfast and saw only white in all directions. They weren't far, she knew that. But her thoughts were on getting home.

About the Author

I spent my early years in a suburb of Chicago before our family moved to Boulder, Colorado while I was yet a teenager. It was a good move for me, and the town and location is beautiful.

During my early years, I was introduced to books – I think every parent pushes their children to read, but I didn't really catch the bug until my High-School years. Afterwards, it was hard for my parents to peel me away from whatever book my nose was in.

I've never been a "good" writer. In fact, I've failed most of my English classes – as may be apparent in the book. A friend of mine constantly complains of my "tense" problems. To date, I still couldn't tell you the parts of a sentence, except for nouns being a person, place or thing.

So… I didn't get any positive feedback from my (English or Creative Writing) teachers growing up, but everyone agreed I was good with computers. So, into computers I went and became a programmer – a very creative career. A career that went nowhere for me.

In my spare time, which I had plenty, I would read. After a while though, reading didn't satisfy my imagination enough and so I delved into writing.

Writing can be very creative, and so different from one writer to another. Complete this sentence and you will know what I mean: "Under the door, I saw a light – when I opened the door …"

… the door slid up into the ceiling – did anyone write that? Then a brilliant cotton candy colored unicorn was revealed. Her name was Tiffany, and she was inviting me to ride her…

… a dump-truck was emptying its content on the floor… It was my kid brother with his toy truck. "Mom! Danny is messing up my bedroom again!"

As you can see, infinite possibilities. Maybe I'll float down a river today, or climb a mountain tomorrow. Or travel on a starship the day after.

I've written lots of stories that sit on my computer, which nobody ever gets to read. Mostly because they are incomplete, some I don't even remember where I was going with the story. What they did for me though, is teach me to write. Good dialog, is not, I looked at Mike's brilliant red race car and asked him, "Hey, how's it going?" but descriptive, "Hey Mike! That's a beautiful race car. How'd you get that color of red? It's brilliant!" At least to me, description through dialog is better than a narrative on the subject.

Writing many incomplete stories can drag you down. I was honestly sick of failing to complete one. So, when I got the idea that became Mermaid Rising, I was determined to see it completed. A little over a year later, the book is a reality. And so, the series continues with more on the way.

65787980R00065

Made in the USA
Charleston, SC
09 January 2017